Looking Glass

Casanova Da Vinci

Copyright © 2017 Casanova Da Vinci

All rights reserved.

ISBN: 1539987647
ISBN-13: 9781539987642

DEDICATION

For my two daughters Chantal & Jade

May your imaginations flourish and bring you joy

CONTENTS

Introduction   *i*

1   *Looking Glass*   *1*

INTRODUCTION

Jack Dawson is a 12-year-old boy that has pretty much grown up his whole life with his Aunt, Milly Dawson, at her country home in the quiet town of Fairydown, Resheen. Having lost his Father at a young age, Jack's Mother, is forced into a deep depressive state through the death of her Husband. Now she searches for a way to deal with her life, as Jack begins to deal with his – whether this is in Fairydown or elsewhere.

When Jack receives a couple of oddball characters appearing in his bedroom throughout his young life, he is finally confronted and introduced to Jaspro Sprig and his hapless friend Norsh Light – Shadow Runners of The Looking Glass.

Taken on an amazing journey through one Mirror to the next, Jack is taken to Spyglass Valley, meeting for the first time the Overseer of the lands: Charadelle – Mage of Light, as well as a few others of the same age with fantastical abilities, and skills.

But with the good, there also comes the bad. Jack's arrival at Spyglass Valley is found to be no coincidence…it was written.

A race of time to save a Creatic Species threatened with death and extinction, Jack, Jaspro, Norsh and all the other Shadow Runners bring together a force more powerful than any Darken Mage could expect, to bring balance and peace to the rest of the land.

"Those days of adventure in Fairydown are the days I miss most as an adult – to be young once more would be Epic."

Jack Dawson
1845

1 LOOKING GLASS

The Shadow Runners

They were called "The Shadow Runner's", though their ability to run through shadow's was not the only fascination about them that had me join their group of Wanted: The Shadow Runner's; gifted with the ability to transport themselves by 'Reflection', or simply by immersing into any 'Shadow'.

Our first encounter came when I stayed at my Aunt Milly's house in Evermore's East End, while the second was at my Cousin Steven's house in Marsham, near Borello. And on both occasions I saw that Jaspro and Norsh had not aged in any way – they were still as young as they were when I was 6 and 11. How could this be?

Having just had my twelfth birthday, Jaspro had come to visit me for what he believed was the very last time. Taking me by the wrist with no reason and somehow taking me to a place I didn't recognize. It kind of looked like a New York postcard; the tall buildings, apartments and skylines that bested the same views and awesome backdrops that proved it was the Big Apple. And, in no way mistaking the Empire State Building.

Jaspro was the leader, maybe, as he didn't get given orders by anyone else that I knew of, but then, there were many things that he kept to himself and didn't tell anyone else.

 'The Looking Glass helps us travel around,' Jaspro said, his sitting up on the very ledge on some very tall building five hundred feet up in the air not causing him any worry. 'Yous be a lucky ones, we will be old soon…then it will close – forever!' He was somehow saddened at the expectation.

 '***Close!*** What do you mean?' I asked making my way over to the ledge to join him.

 'The Looking Glass is only for us young kids yous sees Jack, though I am not a kid, I'm a young man,' Norsh cried out to get in his tuppence worth before Jaspro noisily took over the conversation.

'The Looking Glass is our way of keeping an eye on those that can't stand up for themselves, kind of…here, we'll show you, won't we Norsh?'

With this Norsh stepped forward and took from his pocket a small square piece of glass – it was a mirror. With it he held it out for me to take a hold of, which I did with the thought that they may be pranking me and the glass did nothing at all.

'***It doesn't look special!***' I exclaimed examining it closely.

Norsh and Jaspro laughed. 'That's because you have to say the magic words, ain't it, Jaspro?' Norsh called out with a giggle.

Jaspro nodded. 'Cadabra is the magic word you have to say, or it don't work none, Jack.'

I suddenly remembered that the magic word to the Magicians was similar, not exact, but certainly along those lines.

'***Cadabra!***' I exclaimed, immediately feeling the small square mirror vibrate and pull away from me, but I held it fast.

The whole top of the building that we were stood upon lit up with a very bright light, brighter than my Mum's house lights that dimmed whenever she turned on the TV. Closing my eyes so as not to blind myself, I held out the mirror as far as I could before suddenly, as quickly as the light appeared, it vanished.

'***Cadabra!***' Jaspro and Norsh said in unison, as right before us stood a young girl, she was around eleven-year-old dressed in strange clothing.

'Hello,' She welcomed me with a smile. 'I'd be very careful with that, if I was you?'

Jaspro cut in. 'He ain't the likes of us, Cadabra, so don't you be going and spoiling our fun.'

To me it sounded more of a threat than a request, but for the young girl, she took it lightly for some reason. I had no idea what he meant by his sudden statement that had Norsh taking back the mirror from me with a quick snatch.

'Pity, he looks a lot better than you two…I mean, he looks like he can run better than you two!' She quickly cleared up her mixed words.

'***I want to go with you!***' I shouted up.

Norsh was somehow excited. 'Are you sure?'

I nodded my head and all three started to rush to one another, grabbing an arm each and dance around in circles doing a jig.

'Starlight, Starbright, into the night, bring this child a star tonight. Lift his head to shine with beauty, transport him to his true place of duty.' Cadabra sang out while breaking the six hand circle and surrounding me with Norsh and Jaspro, and then closing me inside where I found I could no longer move.

'What's happening to me?' I yelled to no straight answer.

'The Starlight will decide whether you are ready or not, take the mirror from Norsh and speak your promise into its image. Only then will you know whether you can be one of us.' She spoke with a voice that was somehow enchanting.

Turning to Jaspro I asked him what promise it was that would make me like them, and in turn he spoke along with the other two still dancing around me in a circle.

'You promise fine, you promise true. The things you will see and the things you will do, will stay forever a secret between both me and you.' They chanted.

I took hold of the mirror from Norsh and stared into its dark surround of reflection that found my face, before repeating the words that they had told me word for word. At first the mirror didn't do anything, but then, then it started to move, quiver and then shake in my hand.

'***Erm…Guy's!***' I stuttered.

Staring hard into the mirror I began to see something behind the glass, behind the silver back, it was getting larger and very close to the point of crashing out of the mirror that was still in my hand.

'Think of a place where you have always wanted to be, Jack Dawson…be free…'

My mind immediately thought of the one place I would always wish to be, the only place I wanted to be.

The Way From Paris

I had no idea what happened with the mirror, not until I was suddenly faced with something of a very odd incident. My eyes opened to the break of dawn…in Paris, France!

'How did I get here?' I asked myself aloud and not in my head where it should have been kept.

'Bon Journo, Jack, did you sleep well?' Cadabra asked holding out her hand for me to take so she could pull me up off of the floor. 'You've been asleep for hours.'

Taking her hand I pulled myself up and looked around to see that the sun was rising behind the Eifel Tower, which meant that it was still 4am back in Resheen.

'Very good Jack, but I bet you can't get home before the sun reaches your bedroom window?' She challenged me dryly.

For a moment I stood thinking hard about what Cadabra had said, then thought logically and clearly about accomplishing the challenge by its outright clue ridden statement.

Looking around both Cadabra and myself, I saw a car parked up alongside a Hot Dog Stand, the wing mirrors clearly in my line of sight.

'Before you do this, Jack, you have to know something. If the mirror you use to travel is cracked and never broken, you will be lost forever in the darkness.' Cadabra told me with sadness deep in her voice as if she didn't want to tell me.

'The darkness…!'

'The darkness is the void of Hellencia, home of Salbrinia the evil Sorceress.' Jaspro spoke up appearing behind me suddenly. 'It is said that she helped create the Mirror Port, as a way that she could travel from one place to the other, wreak her vengeance on all of those who opposed her. This is not a place for you, Jack, if you are taken into the darkness, you may never return.'

The story scared the heck out of me – why wouldn't it?

I guess I needed some advice. From Jaspro I welcomed a small shard of mirror that he handed to me.

'Can you help me, Cadabra, please?' I asked walking up to her and handing the small piece of mirror over.

With a long stare into my eyes she took the mirror and turned the reflective side to face me, while with her hand she wrote the word: Redstone into the open air with a single finger.

'Got it?' She asked, just as I looked into the mirror.

'Yes, I've…!' I was suddenly dragged into what appeared to be a cascade of water tides that had sped up by their very fast turbulence. A Jetstream of some sort, it's surrounding ampulets streak racing past me.

Looking down at myself I noticed that I was freefalling, and yet, my whole body felt as if it was resting on something solid, like a table or bed for instance. The fact was I wasn't secured to anything and the faster I traveled, the faster I was starting to see a little white spec becoming larger than life in the middle of someone's living room wall. Slowing to an almost stop I was thrown from the mirror, but not as if discarded in any way. My body bent, folded, turned and flipped until I was placed on my feet facing a couple eating their cereals and drinking their morning coffee while watching the television.

'Oh, hello,' I said with embarrassment.

The couple stopped what they were doing – eating – which gave them a little touch of doubt; doubt whether they were indeed actually seeing me, or whether they were somehow going completely mad.

'Yes, well, I erm…***Bye!***' I didn't know what to say.

Turning around to face their mirror on the wall once more, I thought of home, and in an instant I was back home in the lounge, with the dark sky still above the house outside. I had made it.

Going to bed I slept the remaining few hours before I heard my Aunt Milly's voice shouting me downstairs for breakfast. It was sometimes seen as a waste of time getting me up so early, usually, that is. But today was a great day to see exactly where I could go and how fast I could get there. The adventure had now begun.

Charadelle: The Good

Taking the school bus and arriving to school late came to be quite annoying, as so many of the teachers believed that I had been Dilly-Dallying. It was an unusual feeling for me, too, actually being late marked for register.

'Jack Dawson, why are you in school early?' Mrs. Prech asked while staring down her gold rimmed glasses at me.

'I had my alarm clock fixed, Mrs. Prech.' I replied jokingly. Giving out a slight moan she continued with the register call. From registration to my next lesson, I talked with the friends I had outside in the classroom before seeing something that was very strange in one of the corridors: a bright light radiating from one of the empty classrooms at the end of the hallway. Finding myself entering, there inside was a tall man, middle aged and weathered looking. His eyes were showing an eager, if not determined look as he searched the pictures, the paintings and other posted papers children and teachers had stuck to the walls with cello tape and Blue Tack.

'Are you lost?' I asked walking in on him.

'No, I'm looking for something,' his reply came as he turned to face me. 'I'm looking for Starlight!'

I knew then at that very moment that the man was referring to The Shadow Runner's, and that he must never know what I knew about them. Norsh and Jaspro told me that the Starlight was for those young children, not someone the age of the man.

'*Starlight!*' I gasped. '**Don't you mean sunlight?**'

The obvious attempt to fool the man, though "Fool" may not have been the operative word here, as I was merely trying to take any undue attention from me knowing about anything that he was looking for. He gave a smile that pleaded my attention.

'Do you know anywhere that I can find Starlight, Kid?'

Just as I was about to give my answer the door of the room swung open, it was Jaspro, he was unprepared for the man who had stopped looking at the walls and pictures that hung from them to look straight at Jaspro.

'Blarney stones and Fiddle Sticks, Marlow Watts!' He gasped out a name that he was obviously afraid of, or at the least he was familiar with as this man stared coldly at my new friend.

'*Jaspro Sprig, you is mine, Boy!*' He shouted, taking from

his pocket a small box – a weaponry device of sorts, maybe? Jaspro told me to run, but I didn't – I couldn't.
Watts, the man, pointed the box at Jaspro before walking up to him with quick steps. From the box came a bright light that radiated out like a sphere, its size increasing to that of a wave which had Jaspro clinging to the nearest wall.

'***You is mine now!***' Watts laughed madly.

'***And…You is mine!***' Jaspro exclaimed.

As the light touched Jaspro's face, he began to disappear as if being erased from the reality of the room; his eyes looked at me with a strain, the eager intense glare that begged me to get the hell out of there before I, too, became a victim of Watts. I couldn't do it. I couldn't leave my friend.

'***Leave him alone!***' I shouted my demand at the man.

Watts paused for a moment. 'Two for the price of one, I is on a roll todays.'

Rushing over to the man and knocking the box from his hand, Jaspro was suddenly free of the erasing light, but he was weak. Grabbing my arm he pulled me toward a wall – was I going to hit it hard and hurt myself? No, there, just barely visible was a small Dream Catcher stuck to the wall with Blue Tack, its tiny mirror now glimmered a capture of the sunlight as we both now entered the Jetstream of the Looking Glass. We were free from the clutches of Watts – for now.

The Looking Glass Jetstream brought us both to an empty house, or so we thought. Jaspro was very weak.

'***Who the hell was that?***' I yelped sitting down on a chair to catch my breath for a moment. 'What was that…that **THING** he was holding?'

Told that it was known as 'The Dark Light', though it was of bright light like sunlight, I looked confused.

'The Dark Light, it be the end of us…you, me, all of us who travel The Looking Glass. You saved my life, Jack Dawson, but now you have put the eyes of Salbrinia upon you, too!'

Salbrinia was an evil woman, her anger formed many years ago in the unreachable realms of Dark Light. Her sister, Charadelle, had imprisoned her for her own good – or so the legend tells.

'Who is Charadelle? Is she…an Angel?' I whispered softly.
At the least I expected Jaspro to laugh in my face, but he didn't, he sat down by the side of me and nodded.

'Charadelle is nothing like her evil sister, Salbrinia, and I guess that she is an Angel, of sorts…'

'The Dark Light, does it kill people like us?' I asked.
Jaspro had regained his energy. 'You is a funny kid, Jack, and one who wants to know everything…'

'I am one of you now Jaspro, don't you think that I should know everything that you know, too?'
I could see in his face that he wanted to tell me, but this soon faded as he began to search the room for a mirror.

'First we gets out of here, then we finds us the others. Here, we can use this one. Is you ready Jack Dawson?'
From the room we both disappeared, while from a dark corner a young boy of twelve, maybe thirteen made his way from a closet in the wall. Searching the room frantically he eventually gave up looking to see where we had vanished to.

'***Fairies!*** ' He exclaimed running from the room and down the stairs shouting for his Mother.
Following Jaspro through the Jetstream we arrived at a place that was unlike my world; the sky was a lot darker, colorful in a way that made me feel strange in myself, while around us those people that gathered around glared, whispered and pointed at my unusual clothing. From a large crowd a woman made her way to Jaspro, leading him a short distance away from me to talk discreetly. I could see that he was being asked something with the quick nods, an occasional smile and clear indication that he was listening to her every word.

'This is…!'

'Charadelle!' I spoke for him. 'You're the sister of Salbrinia.'
The woman was quite impressed by my assumption.

'Jack Dawson, the boy from the inner world, welcome to The Crucible,' she smiled.
Charadelle was beautiful, though I very much doubted that she was human – as much as she looked human, she had a glow that set her apart from the likes of me; her white hair that hung

from a jewel encrusted crown, while her clothing was like those of a Victorian – maybe an earlier Bohemian – style, which made me think of some yesteryear Queen…or Princess, even.

'***Inner world!***' I exclaimed puzzled.

Jaspro cut in with a light, but effective cough. '***They're here!***' Turning to face the mirror which both Jaspro and I came through not long since, several men – adults – appeared before us. Charadelle wasn't pleased with their sudden intrusion.

'***Consequences Gentlemen!***' She shouted, her hand lifting into the air and directing some invisible howling force at them. The men battled forward to try and reach Charadelle, but for the power of the force that had them lift off of the ground and spin backwards, back through the mirror. They were gone.

'Jaspro, take our new friend back with you,' Charadelle spoke with a weakened tired breath.

'But you said…!'

Charadelle turned to Jaspro with blazing cold blue eyes and a voice that even had me straightening up.

'***DO AS I SAY!***' She cried out demandingly, before giving a single loud cough and turning away from us.

Jaspro said nothing. He did nothing.

From the mirror came two other Shadow Runner's, two boys, who went straight up to Charadelle and apologized for their lateness. Each of them giving me a second glance.

'They are attacking, Charadelle! Do we summon The…Oh, hello,' the smallest of the young boys suddenly caught sight of me standing there in the crowd.

At first, until Charadelle instructed them to return home, the two Shadow Runner's glared at me with a look of unease.

'He runs with us,' Jaspro shouted to them. 'This is Jack…'

'***Dawson!*** The boy from the Inner World, but how?'

Loris was one of – if not – the youngest of all The Shadow Runners who ran with Calpit and Quendor.

'There hasn't been an Inner World runner with us since…'

Charadelle silenced him with a raised hand. '***Enough!*** Jack is one of us now. Jaspro, take him home and introduce him to the others. Loris, take a message to everyone and tell them to return home…by any means necessary.'

This was an order that seemed hard for Charadelle to make.

Spyglass Valley

Travelling through so many mirrors had me feeling dizzy. On the final one Jaspro had to keep a hold of my arms to steady me into the path of my reflection; it was different somehow to the fact that the face looking back at me, wasn't that of me. It was this that worried me tremendously.

'The last one, Jack, and then that's us – we're home.'

The words spoken by Jaspro soothed me in a knowing that there weren't going to be anymore mirrors, no more running.

Looking up into the place that for Jaspro was home, I was set back with amazement at the sight; buildings like tall temples, rolling hills of color and a town that looked so much like a city.

'Jack Dawson…Spyglass Valley…'

'It's beautiful,' I whispered dreamily.

Giving a smile of pride that any human such as I could call his home by a honoree title given to only beautiful things, Jaspro led me down a long path that would bring us to the first of the many buildings: The Gold Guild Inn – a Tavern of sorts.

'This is where we can find good brave warriors, ones who don't fear The Dark Light's. Here we are safe Jack, nobody will break the spoken words of Charadelle here, not even The Dark Lighters'…or Watts!' Jaspro spoke, his words trailing off into an almost silent whisper.

My attention was taken to the huge valley that the town stood between, while its steep raised hills on either side showed the low bluey-green skylines that brought sunlight spilling over the horizons edge and across each building roof and structure it touched.

'What do we need warriors for again?' I asked turning to face Jaspro, who was still in deep thought with his last statement.

'Because we does, Jack Dawson! Come inside…let me do the talking.' Jaspro replied snapping out of his troubled thoughts.

Inside The Gold Guild Inn, we were greeted by several people

– everyone there in the town was no older than fifteen, sixteen at the best. They stood around tables, sat lazily in chairs, while at a long bar-like counter in front of us kids stood grabbing and clutching at wooden cups from other kids serving behind the bar.

'***Mucky Beer!***' I exclaimed too loudly, as everyone in the place fell silent and snapped their heads around to stare at both Jaspro and me.

'***Mucky Beer!***' One of the kids standing closest to us cried.

Jaspro looked at me with concern. 'You is not a Mage, Jack Dawson, is yous?'

His question meant nothing to the likes of me, but for those others that now shuffled forward toward me, it was that of the question which had me stepping backwards toward the door that both Jaspro and me had just walked through. The feel of fear was washing around in my mouth, that bitter coppery dirt taste that had me gulping hard.

'***Mage!*** No, of course not…do you hate Mage's?' I asked in a shaky voice that had Jaspro break his character of the serious and cautious Inquisitor, to show a rising smile that suddenly turned into laughter.

'I is just messin' with yous, Jack Dawson!' He laughed hard.

Everyone else in the place started laughing, too, except for me, of course. They were so playful, and yet, appeared to be less perturbed by the fact they were at war with The Dark Light.

'***Jaspro Sprig!***' A loud booming voice sounded out over the rapturous laughter – it was Charadelle and Cadabra.

The laughter ceased. All eyes were now turned and focused on Charadelle, who made her way toward both of us, her face showing impatience and disappointment.

'Charadelle, I is sorry, we was just having funs time with Jack Dawson, that's all!' He defended himself.

Raising a hand to Jaspro, Charadelle pointed a concentrated fingertip onto the end of his nose. 'Funs, Jaspro!'

There was nobody in the entire building who wasn't stood with baited breath as to see what was going to happen to Jaspro; in earlier times, before The Looking Glass had taken on those of my services, Charadelle was known to turn humans into little animals, according to legend and myth – and rumor.

   '***Please, Charadelle, it was my fault!***' I cried out suddenly, very much to Charadelle's surprise.
Taking her finger and stare away from Jaspro, she turned and looked at me – right at me with those blue flame eyes as well as a serious face that made me freeze in my movement.

   '***Your fault, Jack!***' She probed loudly, easily seeing through that of my lie.

   'Whatever Jaspro has been accused of doing, it was all my…'
Cadabra stepped forward with an apologetic smile.

   'If I may talk to Jack, Charadelle, just for a moment?'
Charadelle nodded, her eyes still fixed on my eyes, before turning to everyone in the Inn. 'Let them have privacy…***Shoo!*** Jaspro, follow me.'
Everyone left, except for Cadabra and me, we were stood as if not knowing what to say to one another. And, if we did have something to say, then it would be a simple case of not knowing just how to word it right to speak it out loud.

   'Is Jaspro in trouble, Cadabra…for bringing me here to The Gold Guild Inn?' I asked, suddenly breaking the silence.
Cadabra was hesitant on her reply, one which soon brought a reassuring and confident smile to her face.

   'No, Charadelle has a job for him to do before The Midnight Chimes, that's all…is there something that I should know, Jack?' She replied with a question to my behavior with Jaspro.
I shook my head. She asked again, only this time, her tone of voice was different, more demanding. This time I answered.

   'We were…we were recruiting Warriors!' I confessed finally.
Cadabra was surprised, but not shocked by my confession that could have caused many problems for Charadelle and Jaspro.

   '***Warriors!***' She laughed.

   'Fearless Warriors who are neither fearful of The Dark Light, or it's Dark Lands, Cadabra…Don't you see?' I begged her to understand.
The laughter fell to one side quickly, to be replaced with a more serious, grown up look that I recognized only too well

from when my Aunt Milly became angry with me. Cadabra was smaller than my Aunt – smaller than me, even, but she was a girl – beautiful all the same.

'Why don't you go with Jaspro, you know, help him run the errand for Charadelle? When you come back, and if you still want to gather your fearless Warriors, then I shall volunteer my own services to your cause. How's that, Jack?'

The more I thought about Cadabras's words the more I thought the whole thing was a trick, a trapping of sorts that would have me change my mind on facing the evilness that hid behind it's scores of other men and children just like me. Jaspro, Norsh and Cadabra.

'What's the catch?' I asked with a knowing sigh.

It was considered useless the sigh that I gave, because there was no catch, as I put it in Resheenian terms. Cadabra knew that there were limits to my presence in Spyglass Valley, even if I was feeling something strange deep inside.

'Alright,' Cadabra spoke up suddenly, 'if you can travel to The Dark Lands, Jack, then you will prove to me and Charadelle, that you are not just an…Inner World Boy!'

All of a sudden, Cadabras's voice was changed; the young polite girl who I had first met along with Jaspro and Norsh, was now someone who sounded authortive – like my Aunt!

I bowed my head for a moment before looking back up and into Cadabra's eyes, an act that brought something of a chaotic sense around us. I didn't – couldn't – understand it.

'You sound worried, Cadabra, is everything alright?' I asked taking a different approach. 'Is it the town?'

Cadabra was looking right at me, her eyes to my eyes, my eyes to hers. It was somehow intense, exciting, but also scary, too.

'What are you doing?' She whispered softly, her eyes staying focused on mine.

'I'm not doing anything. What are you doing?' I asked as only a stupid person would by asking a stupid question. 'I mean…'

'I know what you mean, Jack Dawson, now stop staring at me and come…!'

I didn't hear her order of taking my eyes away from her,

though I have to admit, when I was drawn into those deep blue eyes of hers, I saw something both remarkable and at the same time terrifying. I don't know how I saw what I did, but I did, and this left only one important question remaining: Did Cadabra know too?

The Dark Lands - Second Visit!

Being careful of what I said, Cadabra lead me out of the Tavern and down through the streets of Spyglass Valley Town, where we stopped outside a small shop, or so I first thought.

'Where are we going Cadabra?' I asked, but received no such answer as I expected.

'*Quickly!* Get inside and lock the door behind you.' She urged me to move faster to avoid anyone's detection.

Clambering inside the building I found it to be a toy shop of some kind, not the sort that my friends or I would visit, but it was a toy shop all the same.

'*Toys!*' I gasped walking back to Cadabra.

She stopped me, of course she stopped me, she was Cadabra, the girl who made Salbrinia disappear into The Dark Lands of Hellencia, wherever that was?

'Let's get something completely clear, Jack Dawson, you are not a person I would trust with this news, but I am taking a chance…!'

I was confused. 'Hang on, you wouldn't…Why wouldn't you trust me? Are you being serious right now?'

The silly words just rolled out of my mouth like there was really no tomorrow, even to the point where Cadabra had to silence me with a firm soft and gentle hand over my mouth.

'*Be quiet! You're babbling, Jack!*' She cried a whisper as soon as she knew I could not respond with speech. 'Can you understand me?'

I nodded a "Yes".

'Good, then let us begin.' She relaxed her hand from my mouth and walked over to a far wall where a quick pull on

some hidden catch opened up the whole length of the room. 'Here in Spyglass Valley Town, we have ways and means of travelling to any destination in the known Star Curtain, except one place, are you with me so far, Jack?'
I was all ears. 'Travelling anywhere!'
Cadabra knew that it was a trick question, though she gave the answer anyway. 'Except The Dark Lands.'
And there it came, almost like a predictable spew of BS that a Car Salesman would give to a responsible adult, but with a lot more attractiveness.

'If The Dark Lands are unreachable, then how are you going to free Salbrinia?' I asked in a dry tone, one which brought back a series of loud indistinguishable remarks that I could not possibly repeat.
Of what I did manage to understand, it was enough to make the decision to leave Spyglass Valley and head home, back to my Aunt Milly's house.
'So, you're leaving, just like that are you?' She shouted after me as I reached for the door handle. '*I lied!* There, now you know…if you want to go, then go…!'
Cadabra was somewhat confusing to me.
'*You lied!* Which part exactly?' I turned and shouted at her.
Cadabra was cut up with the confession, more so for the fact that she liked me, thought that I was cute for a twelve-year-old.
'Charadelle is taking Spyglass Valley to war, Jack Dawson, and if I was you, I would hurry up and decide whose side you're on in this whole thing. Salbrinia is not a good woman…she is a – '
Suddenly from the doorway of the building a tall dark shadow stopped at the front door before knocking four times and then waiting for a reply. Cadabra looked at me while rolling her eyes.
'*Go and answer it!*' She whispered.
Shrugging my shoulders to the point that if anyone should answer the door, it should definitely be the keeper, I finally caved in and hurried over to answer it.
'Ah, you must be Jack Dawson, the new trainee under the wings of Cadabra…Ah, Cadabra!' A man easily in his forty's

stepped inside the building and closed the door behind him.

I had no idea that grown-ups could enter Spyglass Valley Town, or its totalness of a small region equivalent of Resheen – except for Charadelle and those who were non-human.

'Jack Dawson, I'd like you to meet Spiran…my Dad!'

The declaration was a shock, to say the least. Like I said, I thought that adults, or those fifteen or sixteen and over could never enter Spyglass Valley or its majestic town.

'***Father!***' I gulped hard.

Spiran wasn't too hard on me, especially when it came to his only child, Cadabra. He could have punished me with the most painful of methods, but he chose not to because his Daughter was more concerned about the war that was coming.

'What news from the Far Lands, Father?' Cadabra asked rushing over and jumping into his arms.

Spiran looked tired; his face was weathered with age, his hair gray and thinning, as well as his appearance looking drawn and unkempt.

'I must speak to Charadelle, Cadabra, do you know where she is? I've looked around The Volzook, but nobody there has seen her today…'

Before Cadabra could answer her Father, I waded in with a loud gasp. '***The Far Lands…The Volzook!***'

Spiran and Cadabra were surprised, until Cadabra realized that I was neither knowing or familiar with these places that were very important to Spyglass Valley or indeed those of its large settlements of people.

The Far Lands were vast wastelands of The Scorched; miles upon miles of black soil that stretched as far as the eye could see, while those who controlled the lands were The Infected; the unfortunate result of Spyglass's last battle with Hellencia's evil Sorceress, Salbrinia. Resheenian, Fairy, Creatic and Mage fought well in their one hundred and fifty year war against Darkened Magic, but lost hundreds of thousands on each side in total cost of the unfinished war.

While it was The Far Lands that kept a watchful eye over the sanctuary of Spyglass Valley and its people, it was notably that of The Volzook, that made sure no more lives were taken by any planned or stealth sneak attacks brought on further battles with Charadelle's Evil Sister.

'The Far Lands are no place for a…Resheenian Boy, Jack Dawson, or my Daughter, do I make myself clear?' Spiran spoke up in a booming warning voice.

I was scared – terrified even, that Spiran thought me a danger to Cadabra. She, too, saw that the sudden bellowing of her Father was maybe a little too harsh.

'***Jack is our friend, Father, not our enemy!***' Cadabra cried out while taking a hold of his arm to lead him away from me. 'Let's go and find Charadelle, shall we, and give her the news?'

Spiran and Cadabra were quickly gone from the building, I, too, as soon as they left and closed the door was looking into a large mirror while concentrating on my own home. The moment I disappeared into the glass, the door swung open and Cadabra stood saddened by my hasty exit – to her I was gone.

It was the very first time that I'd actually travelled through The Looking Glass Jetstream on my own, something that I should have asked about before taking it upon myself to do solo. The strangeness of the inner vortex of the stream made all of my thoughts wander, as if it was feeding off of them to get me there quicker. As it was, I had only the thoughts of both Cadabra and Spiran's last words fill my head: The Dark Lands, Salbrinia, Hellencia!

Immediately after my cursing of the thoughts popping into my mind and speaking aloud "Hellencia", the entire Jetstream was starting to change color; a deep and dark orange-red, filled with a rich golden light that beamed out and blinded me for a moment before suddenly it disappeared to become replaced by absolute darkness.

'Is this The Dark Lands?' I whispered aloud to myself.

From the ground below me, its black moist and soggy texture, I was spoken to by an effigy, it looked just like a froogon or toasad, but more a froogon.

'Somebody took a wrong turn!' It said hopping over to me.

'***You can speak!***' I gasped, much to the froogon's

amusement.

'Of course, ever since I was two…or maybe three, I forget! My name is Peron.' The froogon greeted its name. It talked!
I don't know how I coped with the shock of it all, though the new found friend told me that I had only lost consciousness for a few minutes, and that when I woke up I screamed only the once. I was glad.

'Am I in The Dark Lands, Peron?' I asked standing to my feet and looking around us both at the darkened vail of what seemed like it was night time.
Peron didn't say anything, it just nodded its head and started telling me what the first thing he was going to do when he got out of there – now that I had come to save him!

'***Save you!***' I gasped with a cough.

'Save me, yes, take me back to…back to…!'
Peron was having trouble remembering.

'***Resheen!***' I blurted in an attempt to help jog his memory.

'No, not Resheen…'

'Spyglass Valley Town!' I shouted out another.
Peron was suddenly in deep thought of the name, and as if he had just remembered it himself, he leapt up onto my shoulder.

'That's it, of course, Spyglass Valley Town. I was taken prisoner by Salbrinia and her soldiers…she was going to…!'
The ground around us both started to shake, gently at first, until suddenly from right under us there came a loud cry of something big! As I walked, sped and ran as fast as I possibly could over the dark and slippery ground to get to a safer place, my footing slipped and I tumbled to the floor. As luck had it Peron had sought safety in my coat so that he wasn't thrown through the air to the ground also.

'***What the heck was that?***' I cried out as the whole ground shook very violently below my feet and then with a huge cracking sound that filled the darkened sky, something resembling a dinosaur crashed through the black soil and onto the surface before us.

'***J-a-c-k!*** So good to see you again!' It too, like Peron spoke out at me as if it knew who I was. 'You should never have

come back, not after the last time!'
I had no idea what the thing was trying to say, but what I did know, was that I'd never been here before. '***The last time!***'
The ***thing*** and Peron both looked at one another with a more than distant look, one that had me feeling strange inside.
The darkness was passing slightly to show a sky of magnificent purple and orange, while across the ground my eyes caught sight of pure black grass, a silty sand speckled with rocks that on second glance towered above me to reveal mountains.

'Is this The Dark Lands?' I whispered to nobody in particular.

'This is not The Dark Lands, Jack, this is Hellencia and again, you should not have returned here. I, Ruber, know that you are in danger if you stay.' The dinosaur actually revealed where I was before introducing itself to my surprise.

'***Hellencia!*** But, it was…'

'The Dark Lands are no place for you, Jack, and neither is that of Hellencia. You have to return to where you came from, or she will find you…she always finds you!' Ruber said with a tone of woe and fear in its voice.
Of course, he was talking about Salbrinia, Charadelle's evil twin sister. And, the fact that I was there carried an equal amount of concern to both Peron and Ruber.

'You have the Looking Glass?' Ruber whispered leaning his long neck down to rest his head on the ground in front of me. 'You have to go.'
Yes, I had the Looking Glass, or a small part of it anyway. Holding it up to my dirtied face I looked into the tiny reflection that had my complete being whipped inside to travel again the Jetstream, and again, for one brief moment I saw not the real me, but somebody who looked just like me – but older.

The Globe

My journey through the Looking Glass worked to a degree, of its soft landings I would certainly rate this one as a 'Fail!'.

'Where have you been?' I heard a voice shout at me. 'Are you

Okay, Jack?'
Having landed on my butt, the pain was coursing through my whole body to my shoulders where I was forced to throw a palm to my mouth "***Ouch!***' I screamed inside my head until it was no longer sore.

'Yes,' I shouted out into the air with a contained second feeling to shout out again, but luckily, it was nothing to stop me from walking from the living room to the kitchen.

There sat at the kitchen table was my Aunt Milly, her head bowed down to scan and trace the letters in the game of "Word Search" she was doing.

'Hi Aunt Milly,' I said making a bee-line for the fridge.

'Have you been to school today, Jack?' She asked, her head hardly raising from the fixed 'Search' position.

The question was a strange one, I had to admit. My Aunt never asked me questions about school, unless she'd had a phone call or letter sent out to her from the Headmaster.

'Yes, and school was fine, Aunt.' I replied pulling open the fridge door and peering inside to see what I could have to quench my thirst. 'Where's the juice?'

My Aunt gave the usual sighs of having to get up off of her seat and scour the kitchen to find the dilute juice, while I sat down at the table and waited quietly and patiently.

'You're Aunt Margaret wants me to spend a few days with her at Marsham, you'll be alright here, won't you, Jack?'

Disappearing and reappearing to and from the pantry, my Aunt brought out the bottle of Summer Fruits and began making me a glass up before handing it to me.

'Aunt Margaret, didn't she pass away last year?' I exclaimed.

Aunt Milly was not happy with my response, not one bit.

'What an awful thing to say Jack!' She cried out sitting down in front of me, folding her arms and giving me a stern look.

'I'm sorry, Aunt Milly, I just thought...!'

The doorbell rang out into the hallway.

'Hold that thought Jack, this will be my new foot spa,' she squealed excitedly, clapping her hands together like a seal.

'I have to go out...to Bill's house, if that's okay?' I spoke up

before she left to answer the door.
Giving a firm confirming nod she held up four fingers; those four fingers signifying that it would be 4 O'clock when she expected me back home, but even for someone like me, it was a little too early.

'Six…Billy's Brother's coming home from Seacliffe today, please!' I begged until her eventual extra nod.

'Okay, six O'clock…and no dilly dallying,' she agreed.

As my Aunt went and answered the door I made my way back into the living room where I looked into the wall mirror and traveled back to Spyglass Valley Town, where to my horror I saw Charadelle and Cadabra standing around a water spring with a young child laying on the floor crying. There had been an attack on the town.

'What happened?' I gasped to the ignorant whispers of those who had flocked around them. 'Was it The Dark Lighter's?'
Nobody would talk to me, not even Cadabra, who on quite a couple of occasions looked over, but then diverted her eyes to Charadelle.

'***Okay, fine!***' I moaned turning around and walking back to the Town Square Looking Glass.

'Maybe it would be better you did go Jack. You are obviously no use to any of us here!' Charadelle called out and paused my steps. A trick that both herself and Cadabra had mastered to a fine art of a T.

The mass gathering of the towns fell silent as they waited for my response, one which they were still waiting for after I had entered the Jetstream of The Looking Glass.

An echo of some kind sounded out within the translucent array of rainbow colors and shades so beautiful, though I could hardly make out the voice to say who it was.

'You can never goes back to The Dark Lands…'
Not knowing how I'd done it exactly, I managed to stop! I lifted my head, arms and legs, to slowly reach a full vertical position within the Jetstream before what I saw for the next few minutes was best described as "Magical".

All around me the Jetstream of The Looking Glass began to

slow down, it's extending rays of greens, yellows and white's came to a motion that allowed me to see that the Jetstream was not what I thought it was. Looking forward I began to see the forming shapes of houses, fields, roads, paths and finally I saw the building structures below a beautiful open sky – was this still Spyglass Valley Town?

'***You there!***' A loud angry voice of a man shouted after me. 'Did you just…did you just shut down The Looking Glass?'
I had no idea what the man was talking about, obviously!

'Where is this place?' I gasped in awe at everything around me and the man who had joined me at the side of a large drum-like hut. 'Is this Spyglass Valley Town?'
The man, short in his tallness and wide in his out breaths was in two minds on whether to approach me, or leave me be to admire the beauty of the picturesque backdrops of Spyglass – the cloaked city of The Shadow Runner's as well as that of Charadelle's empiric temple and palace that stood on a sheer high cliff top not too far away in the distance.

'This is Spyglass City, how did you do that?' The man asked almost in a demanding voice of "Tell me, or else".

'***I stood up!***' I replied, telling him the truth.
Within moments there were more people gathering around me in their droves; news traveled fast in Spyglass, especially when The Spyglass itself had been stopped. I had no idea what I'd done, but, the sudden appearance of Charadelle made it clear that if she was unhappy, then I was in serious trouble.

'Jack, how good to see you.' Charadelle spoke calmly and kindly as if she was really happy to see me. 'How did you stop The Spyglass?'
I didn't know. All that I had done was stand up inside the Jetstream and, well, that was it really. It was difficult to do, but with a little forced strength, it was nothing.

'Is it broken?' I asked turning and pointing up at the hut.
Charadelle was silent, which is funny, because I couldn't remember a time when she was this silent of a catastrophe, as much as the expressions on the people's faces who stood around watching us at that moment in time.

Whispers started up, a few moments later they became louder and more irritating for Charadelle. She looked sad, and yet, she also looked hopeful when finally she looked up at me.

'You stopped The Spyglass, Jack, which means you can also start it back up again, am I right?' Charadelle asked with hope radiating from her voice.

For reasons unbeknown to me I nodded. Charadelle was pleased, as were the others who all began to turn to one another and smile also. I was becoming more scared.

'I mean, as you say, if I stopped The Jetstream, then I should be able to restart it again…if that is what you're saying?' I gave a nervous laugh that Charadelle shrugged away in an instant.

Telling everyone around The Looking Glass to disperse and not to worry, she added that it would be "I" who fixed it.

'So tell me, how do I restart it?' I whispered to an otherwise worried looking young woman.

She knew just as much as I did about restarting The Jetstream, but by working together on the problem, only a team could get the whole thing back to normal again.

'How bad is it, Charadelle?' I asked, eventually reading into the look that she gave as 'Really Bad'.

'The Looking Glass Jetstream reaches out into the whole universe, each beam of colored light touching a point in time. Without The Looking Glass we are defenseless…as are those outside, too.' She replied looking at me as to see that I understood what it was she was saying.

Nobody could go out of Spyglass City, as nobody could come in, either. We were all prisoners within the places we stood.

'Are you saying that I can't go home for tea?' I heard myself question Charadelle in a way she was not accustom to. A frown of anger threw a hand into the air for quiet.

'Until you fix this mess Jack, nobody is going home for tea, or otherwise. Now, tell me everything that you did, start from the beginning…and leave nothing out.'

For more than twenty minutes I stood alone with Charadelle telling her everything that I could remember, except for the one thing that would place a lot of awkward questioning on me

– the echo that I had heard whilst inside The Jetstream.

'There were the normal sounds, too, you know, like hums and beats, that kind of…'

'***Voices!***' She exclaimed suddenly. 'Were there any voices?'

It was hard to lie to Charadelle, nobody knew why they couldn't, while most believed it was some magical spell that she had conjured up and unleashed on the universe.

'I don't remember…Oh, yes, that's right, I heard a voice…!'

I stopped myself with both palms put to my mouth. Charadelle was showing a pleasing smile, while I bowed with shame and that of guilt in not being honest with her in the first place.

'Okay Jack, this voice you don't remember hearing, what exactly didn't it say?' She went about the whole matter another way in which to crush the intense atmosphere around us.

I told her, I explained everything, including the voice and the face that stared back at me within The Looking Glass, the one that frightened me. This was all she needed to know in order to pinpoint exactly what it was that had shut down The Looking Glass and it's Jetstream, both.

'***Margrellin!*** She is here in Spyglass City.'

With this said she turned and looked across the city with a concentrated eye scanning every street, building and structure. A little more than a minute and she had found who she was looking for, and began to chant a tune that sounded so calming and yet, haunting all at the same time.

'She will come to me,' Charadelle whispered in a trance-like tone. 'She will come to me and answer to the people of this city. You will restart The Jetstream and free my people on the outside of The Looking Glass…***Do it now, Jack!***

Pointing into the machine I stepped inside and stood looking up at the roof, its silence deafening to my ears, all the while everything I tried to do to get the thing going again failed.

Sitting down and crossing my legs with frustration, I crossed my arms and put on a dull face. Charadelle was amused in some way, none that I could find remotely funny, however.

Walking over to where I sat she placed a gentle hand upon my shoulder before squeezing me softly.

'The voice of Resheen calls to you, Jack,' she whispered.

'And the voice of Hellencia calls to you, too, Charadelle!' I spoke as if I was none the wiser of what I'd just blurted out.

She smiled. 'You've been there, haven't you?'

It was my time to nod with agreement.

'You talked with…?'

'Peron and Ruber, they were…'

'In your path when you arrived. I know already that which they told you of my Sister, Salbrinia and her dominance over the Dark Lands. But I am curious, I told you not to go there, and yet you did – why?'

It was not my choice to go to The Dark Lands, though to be honest, Hellencia was somewhere far more dangerous. It was in the back of my mind the name, the location picked out by The Looking Glass Jetstream, as to drop me off at the place I had never been. And yet, according to both Peron and Ruber in Hellencia, it was my second visit there – How?

Charadelle turned away to look at two young boys making their way to us, while from the left, a dozen more children marched up and stopped before her.

'There are many things that you don't need to know Jack, but return to Hellencia you must. When you were a young boy, younger than you are now, you were taken to Hellencia from your parents…your Father was killed, your Mother spared and you, you were saved by a young woman who was but a novice beginner taking to The Looking Glass…'

I gasped out loudly. '***Cadabra!***'

Charadelle nodded. 'She entered Hellencia with a true heart and steadfast mind to rescue you from the evil hands of my Sister, before returning back here to Spyglass City. You were so young, so fragile, so…Resheenian!'

That was how I remembered so much and took to The Looking Glass so quickly, but why was I taken in the first place? What did I have that was so special that Salbrinia was prepared to kill me for it?

'Tell him everything, Charadelle, he deserves to know!' A loud voice of a woman shouted out through the gathering crowd.

Everyone who turned to the woman gasped and backed away as she swooned above the ground and stopped before Charadelle. It was Margrellin, and she **was** dressed in the clothes of a princess; her dress and shoulder gown blazen with gold, silver, and pearlescent lined seams that surrounded silk and lace woven finery to fit her slim young body. It was hard to imagine why people were afraid of her, after all, she looked as young as Cadabra, but maybe wiser than Charadelle.

'Margrellin, finally, you came to my home,' Charadelle smiled a strange greeting that had a hint of sarcasm, or so I thought.

'And here you shall stay, Charadelle, how does that feel?' The woman dubbed The Dark Light Sorceress replied dryly.

The two young women stared at one another, and this was when I discovered something of relevance to the two enemies.

'I feel amazed. Such a plan deserves a round of applause for being so...***flawed!*** I may be trapped here, for now, but the way I see it, so are you Margrellin.' Charadelle laughed coldly.

My own thoughts of the behavior between Charadelle and Margrellin were fraught with worry and concern, if it was true of their power and the stories of legend that had been passed through time accounting details of their battles.

'If I may say something, Charadelle...!' I bleated.

Charadelle and Margrellin stopped staring at one another and turned to face me as I plucked up the courage to say aloud what was on my mind.

'You battled before...and you lost. You battled for how many years...and you lost. Do you think that maybe...!'

I didn't get the chance to speak my mind, as Margrellin and Charadelle both, were leaching my memories into their own minds. And though this didn't hurt me physically or mentally, it was still considered an invasion I would have forbade.

'What are you doing Jack?' Charadelle asked with a look of difficulty on her face. My will was somehow too strong for her, and for Margrellin, also, as she fell back with her weakened attempt to read my thoughts.

The Looking Glass, The Jetstream, Spyglass Valley Town and here at the city, it was all connected in some way shape or form by the presence of The Globe; the hut that contained the slip streams junctions and one of several power conduits that were always switched on and never attacked during any oncoming war – not ever.

'What aren't you telling me, Charadelle?' I asked turning to The Globe and holding out a hand before me.

From the inside of the structure a blue luminescent light started to brighten, flicker and spread throughout the center. Charadelle was starting to look pretty perturbed by the way in which The Looking Glass was now powering back up, it's inner Jetstream gleaming it's perpendicular trails of blues, reds and yellows once more, until finally, the whole of The Globe opened up the conduits – left, right, straight on, backwards, upwards and onwards – The Looking Glass was operational.

Turning to Charadelle and Margrellin, I gazed at their eyes if they were my own, seeing into their minds of vast depth, scope and layer; although both tried to stop me from looking into theirs, it was Margrellin who conceded first.

'***Stop!*** Please, I will tell you anything you want to know!'

Charadelle didn't like this. '***You will not!***'

With an attempt to try and use her powers on Margrellin to stop her from telling me anything, I rose a hand and whispered in a low tone, just as Charadelle was about to cast her spell. As if ceased its initiation and build-up of power that she had conjured, it now dissipated into nothing. She was now without her magic powers.

'***What have you done?*** ' She complained loudly looking down at her hands as if it could all be fixed. Margrellin laughed with an annoying smile of victory, a smile that was to last only a few more moments.

Turning to her I lifted a hand to begin chanting, but some strange feeling in the pit of my stomach brought me to stop.

'You can't do it…I'm too strong for you…!'

How wrong she was. With a low nod I gave a sigh.

'You are both hiding something, what is it?' I demanded.

Charadelle was suddenly the one who wanted to do all the talking and explaining, much more than Margrellin, who had attempted twice to do some trickety spell casting to free herself so she could get away – but to where?

'Tell me everything, Charadelle.' I said in a calm soft tone that had her bend and crease with the pain of fighting the power.
It wasn't long before she finally whispered something that even for Margrellin sounded painful: The Mirror Shard Sphere.
Immediately, as soon as she spoke the words my whole body became ingested with a power and strength that had me in a spin; my vision was starting to fail, the heat in my body that much more intense than a fever, while the pulling of what could only be described as 'My Soul' was in excruciatingly pain. It was too painful for my young, weak body to take all at once, and in a moment I passed out unconscious to the ground.

The Midnight Chimes

Regaining consciousness I was welcomed by a worried looking Cadabra, who had seen to it that I was tended to and looked after while I was asleep. She had made sure that I had been taken to one of the lodgings in Spyglass Valley City, more than likely a decision made by Charadelle, considering it was a place that could bring a stop to the war by mechanical disruption and not by an attack.

'What were you doing?' She cried out as soon as she saw my eye lids flick open to look at her.

'Where am I?' I asked searching the inside of my mouth for some form of liquid to quench my thirst. 'What happened?'
Feeling the back of my head Cadabra reached over the bedclothes and took a hold of my hand. I immediately pulled away from her, as if her touching me could do anything like that of Charadelle. I didn't know what she was capable of, and this included Cadabra, too.

'Hey, it's Okay, it's me. Relax.' She assured me that she was doing nothing wrong. 'What do you remember?'
I told her that I could only just remember The Looking Glass going down, and the bright colors that swayed around The

Jetstream to a point where it all went dark. For the benefit of Cadabra, I couldn't remember anything about the confrontation with either Charadelle or Margrellin, which she found odd to say that the spell's I used wouldn't interfere with my memory.

'You took away Charadelle's magic, Jack, how did you do that? Nobody has ever attempted to take away a Grand Mages power…'

'***Charadelle has no power!*** ' I cried rubbing my nervous hands through my hair and trying to get up out of bed.

Stopping me, Cadabra took a hold of my hand and forced me back into the bed before releasing her grip.

'What is it that you all want from me, Cadabra, I mean, is there something that I have that nobody else does? I keep seeing…!' I couldn't say anything else, I had to stay focused.

Asking me several times what it was that I saw, I ignored the repeated question and laid back into the pillow while staring up at the ceiling. Inside my head the inner voice was asking whether I could trust Cadabra, or was she just the same as the secretive Charadelle, or the deceitful Margrellin?

'My Aunt, she'll be worried about me'

'We're worried about you, Jack, don't you see that?'

Maybe she was right, to an extent. I didn't care much for the niceties of hospitality, especially when the Host was herself a composite; barely a human cell in her body, while the rest of her was made up of ninety-nine-percent Witch!

'Where's Jaspro and Norsh?' I asked looking around the room with suspicion.

She told me that they were both away from the city doing an errand of favor for the sake of Spyglass Valley and its people. I found this unbelievable, as Jaspro and Norsh were two of the most unorganized Shadow Runners I'd ever come across. If it hadn't have been for the facts I would have thought that my friend, Cadabra was trying to pull the wool over my eyes.

'The Midnight Chimes, what are they?' I asked, again feeling weak from the power that I was using. Cadabra saw this and yet, she herself found it difficult to rest my urgency.

'Alright, The Midnight Chimes are special church bells, pretty much like Kalsid, Jufolm and Sigweat up in the north. You heard about Balent, it's whole area destroyed in a single stroke from something big…'

'***Balent has fallen!***' I gasped with an uneasy feeling.

For quite a long time I laid listening to Cadabra tell me of The Midnight Chimes, which started out in Borello more than five hundred years ago, but now in today's world, everything but the old traditions had remained.

'The bells are rung in accordance with the old scriptures, and then, when the moon is phased in the correct position, a life of corruption is spoilt. It can be…!'

Stopping her for a moment I asked what she meant by the off-the-cuff-remark. '***Spoilt!***'

'It is our way Jack Dawson, not that of anyone from Resheen, you should know that, or are you going to use that magic you have on me?' She was suddenly scared, I could hear her heart beat banging loudly around in her chest.

'What makes you think I haven't already?' I replied turning my head away and closing my eyes. 'We all love Unicorns, my dear Cadabra!'

I had mentioned something that she now took to heart and with it a leave of silence as she strutted loudly out of the room and into a dim lit corridor. Here she met with Charadelle and Margrellin, who were waiting a few feet away from the door.

'Well?' Charadelle asked impatiently.

Cadabra shook her head. 'Nothing!'

The three women stood pondering on the point of my 'Incursion' as they preferred to call it, a condition of imbalance and infection both, though this I would not notice myself.

'Strange how a Resheenian can come out of bloody nowhere and take the Soul Harp to one of our own, don't you think, my dear Cadabra?' Margrellin purred, but not in a playful manner.

'I think you're wasting your time, time we haven't got to be chasing around after a myth. The Mirror Shard Sphere is neither here in Spyglass, or any other place in the universe, I should know…I saw it destroyed!' Cadabra spoke quietly.

Charadelle was quite interested in hearing the story behind her belief that The Mirror Shard Sphere had indeed been destroyed, more so for the fact of Cadabra herself claiming to have been there at the time.

The Mirror Shard Sphere

Calling in on me the very next morning, Cadabra took me out into the Hospital Garden for some fresh air. Finding a soft piece of grass to sit down next to me, she gave a quick sigh, and then waved Charadelle and Margrellin over to sit along with us while she told us of her adventure.

Cadabra was young, much younger than what she was now, which was unknown by anyone exactly how old she really was. It was the year of flourishing crops in Shellona Town, due east of Spyglass Valley Town, about fifteen day's journey on foot – only seconds by The Looking Glass. The town was modest with only that of a hundred and fifty residents, most of whom worked at the Mine on the south-western ridge that separated all the towns in Chatandra.

'My Father worked as a Steward in the Ore Mines that all of the men worked in by day, digging for Pusanick and Roarstone for trading against food and clothing for the town. What my Father and others in the town didn't see was the change in The Mudrac and their numbers increasing every day…'

I stopped her for a moment. '***Mudrac!*** What is that?'

The Mudrac was a winged beast – Dragon-like - that had escaped from Hellencia when Salbrinia last waged war on Chatandra, in a time that was a million years past to Cadabra.

'The days were shortened by the Majuna's change, the nights even shorter as to the frequent attacks on local villages around the land. But finally the day came when a great horde of Mudrac came and wiped out my whole town of the people, the parents, even the children…except for my Father and me! The Mundrac came and yet, they refused to take us or kill us. I didn't know why until finally we were left alone in the debris.

Those who lived around the town accused me and my Father of being in league with the Mudrac, while those Holy Men of the path claimed I was spared to share my story of what had happened there that day. It was hard to get from one town to the other without some historian announcing my arrival...'

'And that's when you became Cadabra!' I whispered.

Charadelle was somehow looking bored, as was Margrellin.

'The Mudrac have long since gone, many believe that they were cursed by an ancient Mage who banished them back to The Dark Lands, or Hellencia. Nobody knows for sure.' Came a happy comment from Margrellin.

Charadelle, not wanting to be outdone coughed loudly.

'I think you'll find that The Mudrac are small in their numbers from the time that Cadabra is speaking of, though I doubt that they were the reason why she became known as Cadabra. Am I right?' She piped up looking at Cadabra for an answer. 'I mean, your entire town wiped from the face of the universe like that, it would have been easier to climb the great walls of Juzipher and knock on the gates of Orega, wouldn't it, Cadabra?'

The storytelling had me yawn with tiredness, though the way that I was laid with Cadabra nursing my head on her lap was a moment I wanted to remain. But it was late and my Aunt would have phoned Billy's dad to ask where I was and what was holding me up.

'There is a trick...!'

'No, it is not a trick, it is a true measure of the arts in our...or should I say in you, Jack, to best The Looking Glass!' Charadelle broke in on Margrellin's approach to reassure me that everything would be alright.

Brushing my face with a gentle featherlike touch, Cadabra sat up and then rose to her feet, with a little help from Charadelle, who was quickly thinking of a way to prepare.

Asking everyone, including me, to stand well back and get ready for a big show of lights, Charadelle held her hands up in the air and closed her eyes. A few seconds later she was more or less chanting to herself. Nothing happened, not to The

Looking Glass or The Globe. She thought this very strange.

'Lost your touch, my dear?' Margrellin laughed sarcastically. Something was wrong, but not with The Looking Glass or The Globe, it was something that struck me the moment I began to feel weak from my run in with both Mages.

'Who made The Looking Glass?' I asked walking over to The Globe and looking inside. 'Was it a Mage?'

All eyes were on me, as when I turned all three women looked a little suspicious in their silence.

'***Petrius!*** It was a man named Petrius. He was a great man, but by no means was he a Mage, Wizard or otherwise. Why do you ask, Jack, what do you see that we can't?' Charadelle spoke up rocking her head from side to side to see.

The low humming noise coming from The Globe told me that there was something quite not right with The Jetstream; either there was something coming through that was bigger than the streams themselves, or it was something that was going into The Globe at a fantastical speed.

'I have nothing!' I said looking over to Cadabra.

'***Nothing!***' Charadelle cried rushing over to me. 'You ask of the creator, and then you say you have nothing?'

I knew that traveling through The Jetstream would take all those who wanted to go wherever they pleased, but, I also knew that The Looking Glass was not just a portal for the likes of me to enter time present, but also time past.

'The Mirror Shard Sphere, it was destroyed by The Mudrac in your home town, right?' I asked turning to Cadabra.

According to her tale they had attacked the town, taken or killed every man, woman and child, and yet, they allowed both Cadabra and her Father to live. If this was true, then The Mudrac would have had no reason to destroy The Mirror Shard Sphere, unless they were the real Keepers of the object who knew no other way in which to protect it.

'One of them…the biggest of them all, it took The Mirror Shard and ate it. The Mudrac did not burn, it glowed with a radiance I had never before seen. It was beautiful!'

The Mirror Shard Sphere was not lost, it was not destroyed

either, it was ingested with all points and purposes being to protect it – but from whom?

'The Shard, what exactly does it do?' I asked Charadelle, who then looked onto Margrellin for an answer, speedily, too, as by judging by the look on her face she was afraid of me.

'It er...Well, it kind of...I don't know to be honest.'

If it was to be the actions of someone wanting to cower out of telling the truth behind the ancient object, by cower meaning I was sensing some catch to the answer, then Margrellin had to be the winner. '***It's cursed!***'

Finally someone said something that was of use to the whole situation, better that it was Margrellin than Charadelle, but all the more reassuring that it wasn't Cadabra.

'Cursed as in Haunted, you mean?' I gasped.

'A long time ago, my people...'

'***Your people!***' Charadelle yelped with objection.

'Our people...were making their way around Juzipher when they were attacked by two pure black Mudrac's, one from the front, the other from the back of our group. The first Mudrac savaged and ripped to pieces our security, and then came for the rest of us. A man baring an object of great Majesty and beauty confronted The Mudrac and held out the strange object, to which my eyes could not believe what they saw that day. What we call The Mirror Shard Sphere, the man called...The Dark Void. The stranger did not stay around to be thanked, nor was he seen again. I'm afraid anyone touching The Mirror Shard, even just by chance, will be sent on a dark path into the void. And that is all that I know.'

I believed her. Cadabra and Margrellin believed her, too, which was a rising moment of very small celebration.

'Nine-fifty-nine, Jack, it's time you went home!' Charadelle exclaimed quite suddenly and loudly.

The other two women nodded. I was tired, exhausted without the sweats and panic attacks. I needed to rest, but going home and confronting my Aunt in this way wouldn't have made anything any the better. I needed to talk with Jaspro to sort out a couple of things, but that could all wait until tomorrow.

'See you tomorrow?' I waved while turning to The Looking Glass and hitching a fast ride on The Jetstream back home, only not into the living room, but into my own bedroom.

The Myriad War: Light & Dark

The trip back home had in some way brought me back several hours earlier than when I had left, though for Charadelle, she could neither explain it, nor put any kind of theory to the way in which The Looking Glass was behaving. Jaspro, now having returned from his errand for Charadelle sat in his seat within Spyglass's Great Council Chamber.

'That what did happen, is what did pass to the great glass,' he muttered before being stopped by Charadelle.

'Nothing happened to The Looking Glass…nothing that would have altered the time frames for us and Resheen. Worry not, Jack, for The Jetstream is willing enough to save you from a telling off by your Aunt. Therefore, wouldn't it be wise to accept it as a gifted favor?' She spoke in *that* tone again.

I didn't speak out any long winded acceptances, nor did I tell her that The Jetstream had taken me to my bedroom, instead of the one place that it should have. It was a strange feeling in my mind that had me believe that there was something wrong with The Looking Glass, but what that something was, I had no idea yet, but I would not rest until I did.

'The old man on the North Face…!'

Norsh was stopped before he could say anymore, but not enough that I wouldn't ask questions.

The tale which Margrellin told us was one which would put a very big strain over both mine and Cadabra's friendship, as well as Jaspro's, too. As it was there where less than enough Shadow Runner's had to deal with the army that was believed to be growing in The Dark Lands as well as Hellencia itself.

'What old man?' I asked with no surprise at all from the others who were only too prepared to shut Norsh up.

It was a story that both Cadabra and Charadelle had been

avoiding telling me, while Margrellin, herself sat herself down to make herself comfortable before clearing her throat.

'Maybe he should know everything, Charadelle, including the outcome if we fail!' She exclaimed showing a deep concerned look that told me that it was something that I definitely should know.

Charadelle shook her head from side to side, as Cadabra also shook hers. Jaspro's head, however, as funny as it looked bobbing up and down as a sign of a "Yes" vote, I knew that he would soon be made to agree to those older than himself.

'The old man on the North Face, who is he?' I asked.

Nobody but Margrellin smiled. 'He is the one who began The Myriad War, a piece of history that is long since over. Would you like to know the story, Jack Dawson?'

Charadelle looked at Cadabra as if scared by the intentions of Margrellin to tell me, but Cadabra waved an almost still hand at the side of her, to tell Charadelle that she agreed the story should be told. Of course, it was Charadelle who stood to her feet and began to tell it, but not before announcing her reasons of wanting to do so.

'Very well, Jack Dawson, but, there should be no other than me who tells the story, Margrellin, after all, who better to recall the true story than me? Are you ready Jack, to hear the one story that each and every one of us here in Spyglass Valley fear?' She spoke with a hint of anger in her voice. 'The Myriad War was brutal, destructive and most of all, it was an unjust course of action that could not be made simple by the passing of days, weeks or even months. You see Jack, The Mirror Port was considered too special by anyone to try and destroy it, even my Sister, Salbrinia knew of the painful consequences of messing with The Looking Glass. It's great potent properties, some that you, like us, have endured during our time here in the valley; your thoughts in variant cascades of vision, your heart stronger, strength and speed faster – your whole body changing to the ways of The Jetstream. The old man on the North Face of Juzipher is called Talon, the appointed guardian of Hellencia and Gate Keeper of Orega, the Black Mountain

Temple.'

The story was wowed by us all, even a look of great pride in telling us the story showed in Charadelle's eyes. The storytelling was so intense to my thoughts that I could actually see both Juzipher and Orega as clearly as I was seeing everyone around me; the dark sky above Juzipher was an almost neon blue, the ground like I remember it except for fire spots that speckled their way across jagged gauges and crevices. That place looked like a hellish land that even I would hate to travel. This was a story that brought the face of the old man of the north – Talon – close to view from a dark shadowy profile. He was looking out across the whole kingdom of Hellencia and far beyond The Dark Lands, his sights set on somewhere other than there on that cold, dead and lonely mountain.

'The old man of the North Face, he is old!' I whispered my thoughts aloud, enough for the others to hear me.

'***You can see him!***' Charadelle gasped rushing over to my side and crouching down. 'Can he see you?'

I looked right at the old man, his cloaked robes with a dark raven colored hoodie concealing half his face from me, but yes, I could see him, as for him seeing me, there was no possible way. My description of him was intriguing to Margrellin, who glanced over to Cadabra with a warm smile.

'He seems to be staring out at something from the top of Juzipher...***Spyglass!***' I suddenly called out.

Charadelle calmed me with a soft gentle squeeze of her hand on my arm, her voice sounding strange as she spoke to me.

'The man on the North Face is right next to you, can you see him?' She whispered softly.

I looked to my side and sure enough the man was there, but his face again, I couldn't see fully for the hoodie that hid it.

'Slowly, I want you to walk around and get in front of the man, can you do that, Jack?' She asked with a hint of caution in her voice this time. 'Face him and let him know you are of no danger to him.'

Doing as Charadelle asked me, I slowly made my way around to the front of the old man, before stopping and turning to face him. What I saw and what I could only just stare at in complete shock and awe, was the face that looked back at me with sadness, pity, even empathy. That face was me!

Snapping out of the relaxed hypnotic state that Charadelle had somehow put me into, I became filled with a zillion emotions which knocked me into the middle of next week and back again. Charadelle looked at me worried, as did Cadabra and Jaspro. As for Margrellin, however, she looked aware of the whole situation. Did she know that the old man of the North Face was me all along?

'The Man of the North Face is coming to Spyglass Valley, whether we like it or not, we must prepare for his arrival.' I informed everyone before quickly becoming weak.

It was the way in which I spoke that had Charadelle turning to Jaspro and Norsh, for them to go and bring every capable hand that was prepared to fight. I turned and demanded them to stay where they were, something that Charadelle did not like or appreciate being demanded in front of her people.

'You stand on your own self-worth, Jack Dawson, be warned, you only have favor because of who you are…'

'And who is it that I am, Charadelle? **Who am I?**' I screamed out at the top of my lungs. '**Do you know who I am?**'

Everyone in the chamber fell silent while Charadelle scoured her mind to think what it could possibly be that had me so irritated and beside myself.

'You are Jack Dawson, the Inner World Boy,' she replied to the shaking of my head. 'You're not Jack Dawson? Or you're not The Inner world Boy?'

If I could have explained everything there and then to them all, then I would have done just that, but as it was, we were pushed for time before The Man of the North Face came to reveal his true identity – an identity that would surely come as a shock to everyone I had met and become a part of over the past few days. I was scared, too scared to stay, and yet, too scared to go.

'The Man on the North Face, Charadelle, it's…'

I was rudely interrupted by Margrellin, who gave a loud cough before walking to my side.

'The Man on the North Face is on his way, Jack Dawson, so I would advise you to go home and stay there until such a time as Charadelle needs you. Would you not agree, Charadelle?'
Charadelle was reluctant to agree, but she did so anyway to the sound of the alarms across the Valley mountains and hills.

'Go home, Jack Dawson, and stay there until I send word.'
And that was that. Charadelle led Cadabra and Jaspro away, as well as Norsh and Margrellin, who looked back discreetly and gave a very unsettling wink as I entered The Looking Glass and made my way home.

Salbrinia: The Bad

Waiting for a bus was considered longer than waiting for a full kettle to come to the boil, but waiting for word from Spyglass Valley Town, or it's city, was far longer than either the bus and kettle combined. I was becoming restless; thoughts of going back through The Jetstream to Spyglass had been taunting me all morning.

My Aunt had gone to visit my Aunt Margaret in Fairydown, so I was on my own in the huge house. The second thought of this fact had me search my mind of all sorts; I could do anything while Aunt Milly was not there, like eat and drink as much as I pleased, watch as much television as I wanted, go to bed when I wanted and have full run of the house, its attic, its cellar and all the grounds. But this would have been pretty much the same with Aunt Milly there, too, I guess.

'What are you going to do to pass the time?' A strange voice called out to me.

I looked around me but couldn't see anyone. Again, a few moments later and the voice called out again, only this time, I was confronted by a young girl who looked a few years older than me, and she was beautiful.

'You look bored, Jack Dawson, how would you like to play a game?' She asked with an expectant smile.

A game would be good, I suppose.

'What do you want to play?' I asked sheepishly.

'Hide and Seek, I'll hide and you seek, Okay?' She declared with a look of determination in her soft green eyes.

I shrugged my shoulders. 'Okay, but only in the house!'

This seemed to dampen the excitement a little.

'But The Jetstream, Jack! You want to go back into The Jetstream, don't you?' She spoke in a tone that appeared to enchant me, making me feel relaxed and all warm inside.

Of course I wanted to go back into The Jetstream, I wanted to go everywhere there was to go in the whole known universe.

'Alright,' I agreed, 'but not too far, we don't want to be getting lost, do we?'

The girl smiled. 'That's the spirit, Jack Dawson. My name is Sensteris, are you ready to play?'

Nodding my head I turned away from her and began counting out loudly from one, and when I had reached one hundred, I turned to find Sensteris was gone. Looking around the room to find a mirror, I was distracted by a strange sunlight reflection that shone intermittently through the living room window.

Rushing over to the window I looked out at the gleam, it was from a small piece of mirror glass that one of The Shadow Runners was holding in their hand to get my attention. Joining them outside in the garden I found it to be Loris, he was injured pretty badly.

'**Loris!** What happened? Where are the other's?' I asked to an exhausted young lad who had been hit in the stomach with some strange weapon. 'Is the war over yet?'

Loris struggled for breath. 'Charadelle has fallen Jack!'

At first I believed he had not finished speaking, that he was going to tell me that Charadelle had fallen, but risen again to defeat the Dark Light. He lowered his head instead and said no more of Charadelle.

'Maybe you should go back, Jack Dawson, make things right?' Sensteris whispered suddenly appearing behind me and now facing Loris's scared face. 'Hello Loris!'

'**Salbrinia!**' Loris gasped trying to scramble away from us both and take out his mirror to escape. I stopped him.

'**Wait!** I mean you no harm, neither you or Jack are in any danger here, Loris – not yet anyway!' Sensteris, who was now Salbrinia called out to him.

The moment was as strange as coming face to face with that something or someone that you knew only too well was evil, but you stood refrectless anyway. For Salbrinia, she was stood with a convincing smile on her face, while I was in denial and smiling cautiously.

'Spyglass Valley has fallen, Salbrinia, isn't that what you and The Man of the North Face wanted?' Loris screamed out as he fell to his knees to the floor and sobbed at his loss.

There was no reaction given to his sudden outburst, both myself and Salbrinia knew that it made no difference now what people thought of her, whether evil or otherwise.

'The Man of the North Face is nothing to do with me, Loris, I can assure you of that.' Salbrinia spoke out in a moderately polite fashion, just before stepping back and away from us both. 'You'll need the speed of a Rudikin, and the strength of Karondemoose and the luck of…well, you get the picture, don't you Jack?'

I didn't quite know what she meant by all the things she said, though the Rudikin was somewhat a giveaway as to the soup and vegetables that Spyglass Valley Town offered to everyone who was needing strength of some kind.

'**Rudikin Soup!**' I exclaimed with a grimace that sent both Loris and Salbrinia howling out with laughter.

'You certainly are a strange one, Jack Dawson, tell me, the world that you come from, does it have Rudikin?' She asked between her laughter.

I thought for a moment. 'What does it look like?'

Loris grabbed my attention with a quick whistle before he threw me a small leather pouch, which I caught with a single hand by catching it in flight, much to both mine and the Loris' surprise. Opening the pouch I found it to have been filled with damp, moist meat segments.

'That is Rudikin, Jack, go on, taste it!' He encouraged me.

Taking a small piece of the meat-like food I bit into the soft, melt in your mouth delight, it's taste and texture becoming that of a favored choice of any food.

'He be liking that, Salbrinia, he don't know what Rudikin looks like, but he certainly knows now what it tastes like.'

Loris laughed hard. The meat was delicious in every sense of the word, but it had me sit down on the grass as if I was tired.

'*Oopsy! Ah, right…!*'

'*Stand up Jack, don't lie down!*' Salbrinia advised me quite sternly at first, before rushing to my side and pulling me up off of the ground. 'Rudikin is a very fast paced Creatic, it's hidden properties, however, they're slightly reversed.'

Salbrinia was trying to tell me that the Creatic or animal-like creature as they called them in Spyglass, was used as a sleeping supplement that was used on Sherack's from the North Provinces of Spyglass and beyond.

'I feel so tired, Salbrinia, I don't think I'm going to…' I yawned out an incomplete statement that was to say I was no longer any use to anyone.

'You'll be fine, Jack, you need to walk around…it doesn't stay in your system long, just long enough to be able to use it as a quick getaway.' She told me in an attempt to put my mind at rest, but didn't really, because now I was feeling myself drifting off into a subconscious soothing dream; the whole entire garden where I was stood facing Salbrinia, now gave way to a mountainous range of skyward clouds and low banking mist that tickled the tops of peaks, scars and gauges. It was daytime, the sun was high, the air soft, warm and ever so pleasant while surrounding me.

Inside my head I could hear Salbrinia shouting questions to me over the sound of a very loud ringing – a bell!

'I can hear a bell. The temple!' I gasped making my way forward without further thought of how I was going to get there. Nevertheless, I got there.

Somehow I knew that I'd already been here before. Salbrinia shouted back again, telling me not to go anywhere near the Orega Temple, that it would be dangerous to even step a foot upon its darkened steps for someone like me – Resheenian.

It was too late to pull myself back or stop myself for that matter, I was virtually there at the foot of The Orega Temple.

'And who have we here?' A loud booming voice asked.

'I am Jack,' I replied with a smile.

Before me stood The Man from the North Face.

'*My! My! My!* How I have grown since…since I grew up!' The older me spoke out surprised.

The feeling was one which I couldn't understand; there was no fear, no hesitation, no doubt, just an overwhelming feeling that I was safe. The Man of the North Face – Me – as far as I could see, had no intentions of hurting me.

'Spyglass Valley, did you destroy it?' I demanded, much to my older self's objection.

'Spyglass Valley is…I cannot say, but it just *IS*, now go back and tell them they are not safe there, Jack.'

In a moment of blinking my eyelids closed and opened again, I was confronted by Salbrinia and Loris, who towered over me.

'Is he deaded?' Loris asked prodding me in the cheek with a nibbled finger of grass wheat and charcoal.

'No, of course not, he would have turned blue by now. Jack, can you hear me?' Salbrinia replied stroking the side of my face with a gentle hand.

As soon as my eyes opened I knew that I was no longer at Juzipher Mountain, or The Orega Temple where The Man of the North Face stood. A moment passed before I finally gave a reply to Salbrinia's question.

'Yes, I'm fine. He…I mean, I talked to myself on Juzipher, I warned myself, but it doesn't make any sense!' I babbled.

Helping me to my feet Loris told me to calm down before Salbrinia pointed out that the Rudikin meat could not be ruled out on having caused trickery visions, though she already knew, as did Loris, that what I had described to them both was not an illusion brought on by the food.

'Something is attacking Spyglass, and it isn't what everyone believes it to be!' I blurted out while submerging myself into deep thought. 'The Rexana from the North Province shares a piece of land with those Sherack's, but, if Sheekan's could have

somehow made it through the mountains…!'
Salbrinia started clapping her hands together loudly, slow at first before then applauding my working out the danger that was heading toward Spyglass, the town, the city, the whole Province.

'Well done, Jack Dawson, but now we need to discover a way to send them back…*or get rid of them!*' She smiled with a proud look on her face.

I was in no shape to go chasing Sheekan's, or any other Creatic for that matter. And by the look on Loris's face, too, he was probably contemplating taking that piece of glass from his pocket and jumping into The Jetstream.

'*We have to travel!*' I exclaimed suddenly.

Salbrinia stopped smiling because she knew exactly what I was talking about – where I was talking about going.

'*Hellencia!* But why, Jack, there's nothing there that can help us get rid of the Creatic's?' She asked in an almost demanding voice that scared both Loris and me.

'It is the only place that The Sheekan's will go!' I replied with a knowing look on my face. 'A friend of mine has a dad who works at U. R. Future-Technologies in Seacliffe, he says that those Sheekan's in Resheen are from somewhere else – somewhere else being Hellencia, of course, but you already knew that, didn't you?'

My directness of the truth was accepted strangely, but all the same it was accepted by Salbrinia

'The Sheekan's came from many places, Jack, not just The Island and Resheen, but lots of places. Did you know that a Sheekan of just eighteen Sun Cycles can travel to places that nobody else can?' She began telling us of the fierce Creatic's that were able to destroy any small town that it had set in its path, except one in the north of The Island divide – Nasperine. Salbrinia made her way over to a small fence that overlooked the largest of the fields in Resheen, while lifting a slow hand to point, until turning it in various directions before her.

'The Sheekan's are very proud Creatic's, Jack, they can even be loyal to all our races, if we showed them some respect. It was a Man not long ago for me, who killed the very first Sheekan and took it back to his village to show his ruler the spoils that they brought with each kill. It was a Mantehorned Sheekan, one of the very first, and unfortunately one of the very last of its origins. Man had killed what the Sheekan did consider their leader…Their Queen!'

This was a scary story, even though there were no talk of violence or death about its tale, I couldn't help but feel sorry for that Sheekan. Loris, too, had had quite a scare from the story Salbrinia told.

'Then why did he kill the Creatic?' Loris piped up suddenly.

Salbrinia turned and gave a strained smile. 'Because they didn't know what the death of The Mantehorne would bring, it was seen as threatening to them and as with all threatening things Resheenian's killed it without any provocation.'

It was seemingly barbaric of any ancestral family member to have gone through the times of The Myriad Wars so long ago, especially with much less the weapons to ward them off.

'If you said and she agreed, then how many of these Sheekan's are we going to be greeted by in Hellencia?' Loris asked with burning curiosity.

It was a fair question that he was asking, one which deserved a fair answer without deceit or lie.

'There will be many, Loris…'

'But how many, exactly?' He threw another question at me.

I puckered up and became relaxed. 'I don't know exactly, but I'm sure there'll be plenty for us all to share.'

Salbrinia was finding the questioning rather entertaining, to say that she was only too familiar with Hellencia, it being her home.

'There are more than one thousand sets of parents, each set carries and delivers up to five infants. An Infant can grow a foot per Sun Cycle, while the Parents become the Guardians of these Infants – One big nice vicious family. Of course, that was more than two hundred Resheen years ago.'

Salbrinia purposely left out the last count until the end in the hope that we would be comfortable with the amount so long

ago, which would have been very true.
It was too many Creatic's to be getting into the middle of a fight with, even if we had the numbers to fight them all.

'Have you not been listening, Jack?' Salbrinia cried out.
I didn't understand at first what she was trying to tell me, if anything at all. But then it clicked into place so obviously.
Stopping me from saying anything with a raised finger in the air, I nodded silently to confirm I understood.
Standing together in a small circle, Salbrinia, Loris and me took a hold of the small piece of mirror that Loris took from his pocket and held it out in his hand. With one final glance around we disappeared into The Jetstream.

The Dark Lands - First Visit

With the thought of emerging from the same piece of shattered shard as I had after last leaving Spyglass Valley, my eyes were greeted with a sight I had never seen. Before me was a colossal ancient Temple.

'This is Hellencia, my home. Welcome back Jack Dawson.'
The greeting was sounding almost rehearsed in the sense that Salbrinia wanted me there. Was this a trap?

'The broken shard of the waste lands...!'
'You have been here before, Jack?' She said with concern in the fact I had been there before this moment.

'The two strange Creatic's, Peron and Ruber, I told you of them back in Resheen...!'

'I don't understand!' Salbrinia gave a quiet gasp.
Something was wrong! Suddenly, both Salbrinia and Loris looked at me strangely. I was so confused.

'The Jetstream, it can sometimes do things that reset those memories of other travelers Jack, don't worry, if there are Creatic's here baring those names, then we shall seek their help when the time comes.' I was reassured by Salbrinia before she led us onward to the Temple.

It was quite a long walk through the dark jagged mountain

passes to the foothills, to the steps that would lead us straight up and into Salbrinia's home, a place she had been made a prisoner of so long ago.

'The Waste Lands are too far to travel on foot from here, so I will make arrangements for us to be taken by Glimf. But we'll have to rest and have food first...'

I stopped her with a discourteous interruption that had her staring down at me so hard and deep, that at one point I could have sworn that I saw the Pits of Vorelee in them, its power almost initiating The Tremadale.

'We have no time to stop and rest, Salbrinia, we have to get out there and meet with The Sheekan's, before they destroy the entire Valley...and what's a Glimf?' I yelled out.

Salbrinia laughed. 'Is it because you think you cannot trust me, Jack, or because you don't know if you can trust yourself? We all have a darker side, you, Loris, even my Sister Charadelle, who neither of you have mentioned once since we met!'

Coincidence, lax of memory, or just plain ignorance were three of the possible reasons we didn't bring Charadelle's name up in front of the one person who'd been banished by her command. Could we have been in mind of anything else other than them, then it was highly likely that The Jetstream glitch that Salbrinia mentioned upon our arrival may well have erased it from our thoughts.

'I trust nobody, but I do speak the truth – ***always!***' I hissed as I walked past her through the large Temple doors and into a huge open hall that had a single neonic blue staircase climbing up as far as it could go to the very top of the Temple spire. The sight was amazing, even for my young innocent eyes of Resheen and simplistic structures.

'I think there should be a few words passed around all of us here, just so that we all know where we stand in all of this...I don't even know what all of this is, to be honest. But you'll see, Jack Dawson, just how wrong you can be!' Salbrinia sounded off at me with her appeal from the more sensitive side of her deepened personality.

Clicking her fingers there was a loud knocking sound coming

from in front of us to the right of the stairs, where here a small door opened up and allowed several tall men holding silver trays to enter the room in a strange formation.

'Food, you'll all need it for where we're going!' She laughed before making her way to a second door to the left and quickly disappearing inside.

Loris walked up to me, his quietness throughout our journey since hearing the bad news of Charadelle and Cadabra was now beginning to sway me to my original plan of action.

'Do you trusts her, Jack Dawson?' Loris asked.

Without turning around to face him I nodded my head. 'No.'

He never mentioned it again after that, probably because his own judgements were not that far from my own.

'Food Gentlemen!' The men holding the trays announced as they greeted us with meats, sweets and treats all in generously large portions, too. It was hard to resist the indulgence.

While Salbrinia was away doing her thing, Loris and I made ourselves a Hanishkawow Delight; a sprinkle of many treats that would rot the shine from any young tooth, while based with a place and serve of Cariffo Cake and sauce. The final touches of a Sprig Lemon and Nirnroot Blade gave the whole thing a delicious glow.

'*My Gods!*' Salbrinia's voice called out loudly as she returned from the door, holding in her hand a small black case. 'Are you two going to eat that?'

Loris looked across at me with a "Just caught" expression.

With a pointed finger Loris panicked. '***It was Jack's idea!***'

I couldn't believe it for a moment, until I realized something that was equally, if not more important to the quest that we were now on to save Spyglass Valley.

'You said we needed to eat, to gather our strength and get ready to face The Sheekan's…!'

'I didn't say eat treats, did I?' She said as a matter of factly. 'All that sweet stuff will slow you down.' Salbrinia said turning to the men who served us the food. 'Bring them something for the journey…proper food, or I will be serving The Sheekan with your heads upon those trays.'

Her warning brought fear and quickness to each their step as they rushed back to the door on the right and disappeared. As for Salbrinia, she crouched down in front of me to place the black velvet covered case on the floor, just as she opened it to the low gasp of Loris.

'This is the Scepter of Storms, probably the most powerful weapon in all of Chatandra. The Roarstone was cut over the thousands of Resheenian Generations, and just as many of our own kind, too. This can make all the difference to our cause…'
I had to remind Salbrinia that this was not a 'Cause', it was that of a 'Quest', important to her or not, but very important to me. The Scepter of Storms was a very powerful weapon, as she had already pointed out, and yet, what she left out was the fact that its unstable Roarstone was placed and set more than two or maybe three thousand millennia ago.

'I assure you, Jack, it will do what we need it to do. Now, if we are all ready, I will take you to the Glimf. This way.'
Salbrinia turned and faced the staircase before starting to take each and every one of the steps, the steep climb making all of us tired and exhausted by the time we reached the top flight.

'Blarney Stones and Elven Leaves, isn't there another way to get up here without all of those big stacked boxes?' Loris gasped his last breath before collapsing down on the ground.

'You seem lost without your Creatic abilities Half-Light!' Salbrinia taunted Loris, insulting him with the term "Half-Light" very much.

'I could still…I…I would…Oh, never minds,' he screamed with his eyes showing anger and sadness both.
Cutting in between them both I faced Salbrinia and gave her a scolding look of dissatisfaction at the way she had spoken to Loris. I don't know if she meant what she then said to Loris, but at this point of the journey, they both had to keep their distance from one another.

'My apologies, Loris Twinkle, I had you mistaken for some other…well, yes, I'm sorry.' Salbrinia said sincerely before she fell into deep thought.
From where we were standing on the top flight of stairs we

could see something sparkling below a roof of glass above our heads, this was where The Glimf was, its two-toned black into grey enameled paint over a colossal sized Airship was absolutely awe inspiring, to say the least. It's huge gas filled body bulbous to the points of each wall around the room we stood, while underneath the fuselage a Command Module sat with many of Salbrinia's Private Guards, and two others: Peron and Ruber.

'That's the…' I stopped quickly, my attempt at pulling back the words already spoken to give away my noticing of the two Creatic's that I had met before. 'I mean, that's an amazing balloon, Salbrinia.'

The suspicion in her eyes told me a lot about the young woman taking us to The Dark Lands, so much so, that I even wagered her an arrangement: Get us to The Dark Lands safely and in return, she would have her freedom from Hellencia.

As if telling a joke to everyone, she began to cackle a very annoying laugh that made me doubt her allegiance to us.

It was now that I asked her what was so amusing?

'Hellencia is not my prison, Jack, it's my home…mine and my Sister's. What you are offering me is worthless to the fact that in this realm, you have no magic, no abilities, only the wits and skills you enter with freely of yourselves. May I ask who it is whose teaching you all over there in Chatandra, because there certainly isn't any knowledge of my existence!'

I was almost believing Salbrinia's words for our amusement before boarding the large airship and getting on our way. Deep down, however, I couldn't help but feel she was being honest.

The Captain of the craft was William, who was no older than fourteen or fifteen, his steady hand and watchful eyes on our ascent to the glass roof was quite remarkable, especially as the roof was still in our way from exiting the top of the building.

'Permission to ascend to The Dark Lands, your Majesty?' He asked with a brief bow.

Salbrinia raised a high hand that immediately sent a small flash spore of light into the air and across the whole structure of glass roofing, before suddenly vanishing into thin air. The spectacle took only a few seconds to complete, but complete it did before we could in any way collide with the glass.

'***Awesome!***' Loris gasped staring at the neonic white bright tint of light that span around to hold apart the panes while we elevated into the night sky and finally started on our way to The Dark Lands, the most treacherous part of Hellencia, next to The "***Schloppoloppa Pits***" to the deep south.

'What happened there?' Loris asked Salbrinia inquisitively.

'Well, my dear Loris, it is The Schloppoloppa Pits of the south that creates the heat that powers the lands and restores the damage that all Chatandrian's make...kind of like a Maintenance Guy who is never seen. You don't seem that very well educated Loris, maybe you should...!'

I couldn't take her being so cruel to Loris. '***STOP IT!***'

Salbrinia was shocked with my outburst, as was that of Loris and William, too. The warmth from the embarrassment began to heat up my cheeks as I stumbled with my words.

'Can't you see his scared...tired, even...he's only young and you are...**Come on!**' I tried to gather the right words together, but again, there was something not right about this whole thing, whether it was The Jetstream, The Looking Glass or even both, I was starting to get a really bad feeling in the pit of my stomach about this whole Quest.

'Alright, Jack Dawson, I will leave your little friend alone. You have my word. Tell me, my Sister, Charadelle, where does she sit in all of this war?'

The question was not valid, as she knew only too well that her Sister was of Good, not Evil like she was. But, as she happened to ask, I thought how her hurtful words upon Loris had upset him so much, that now he would not go anywhere near Salbrinia. It would be only fair to put her back in her place, wouldn't it? For the whole journey I told of how Charadelle had saved the children from many disasters, taken them under her wing – so to speak – and kept everything running smoothly in Spyglass Valley. For sure I thought that Salbrinia would be bored...but this was not the case – she was proud.

The Bad Lands

Turning to William, Salbrinia asked him for the co-ordinates to The Sheekan Camp, for which William informed her that it was no longer a camp in the holds of The Bad Lands, but that of a city. Salbrinia was not so pleased with the information.

'***City!*** Do they even have fingers?' She exclaimed suddenly.
The point now was they were organized to an extent, which would also mean that they were somewhere in the process of being civilized, too, maybe! William engaged our descent to the dark ground, bringing the Glimf to a very soft landing.
Disembarking from the Glimf, as if from a plane, we ventured out onto unfamiliar soil; its darkened scorch making it crackle and break under our light footed steps, while before us and all around us, too, blackness was speckled with signs of recent activity.

'There are tracks…lots of them, pretty fresh too by the looks of them. I'd say we are… ***Uh Oh!***'
Just then from all around us, from the darkness of the ground and darkness of the sky, squillions of Sheekan's opened their eyes – the speckles of activity were not from a latter sense, but a current one. They had been hiding, lying in wait for those who happened upon their land.

'Excuse me…coming through…thank you…' Peron and Ruber made their way through the small crowd of Hellencian Guards to stand in front of us all, a quick clearing of their throat made before they called out to the Sheekan's. 'We come with arms open and a message for your…your…!'
Peron was finding it difficult to find their Rulers name, while Salbrinia, too, was busy trying to think. The air seemed more denser, positively thicker than that of Spyglass Valley and my home, but it would never occur to any of us at that time, that in the distance of all our native Sheekan's, something was sucking away the natural air and atmosphere of the land.

'Let me try,' Ruber suggested taking his place in front of Peron and facing the many Creatic's. 'We are here to address the wisest of your colony…'

Suddenly, from the ground below us the loud sound and tremendous tremor of a dull thud and rumble of the scorch soil began to heave itself apart. Moving backwards, slowly at first, until eventually picking up our speed to escape the towering skyward land rising and falling to and fro to the ground around us. If this was the wisest of all The Sheekan's, then it was big!

Salbrinia was the first to stop and turn around to see if it was safe for everyone else to stop, it was, but for where we stood when addressing the Creatic's, the whole area was now just one huge bottomless hole. Exactly what stood on the far side of this hole, though small to The Sheekan Hal that stood there, we saw something new.

'You have much courage coming here to The Bad Lands, you and your kind are killing us…are you here to kill us…Jack Dawson?' The huge majestical Sheekan asked us in an almost creepy voice sounding like a Resheenian voice.

The Sheekan directed the question at me, but why? I had never seen anything like this particular one, as all the others were so rare in Resheen, as they now were in Spyglass Valley, too through their declining numbers.

'My reasons of being here are to offer you a safer place to live, not to kill you.' I shouted out loudly so that it would hear me. This it did and immediately swooped down its head to stop within inches of my face.

'*Safer place, Jack Dawson!*' It spoke with a voice so loud and a breath that had me dig in my heels to the ground to stop me from falling over backwards. 'You are not Resheenian, you are…?'

Salbrinia stepped forward quickly. '*Enough!* We are here to see The Seeker, bring them to us and we will talk about your immediate surrender.'

This was not the plan that both myself and Loris had, it was a coup that would bring The Sheekan's to a new level of anger from Salbrinia's words.

'What are you doing?' I demanded pulling Salbrinia away

from the Sheekan. 'We came here to save these Creatic's, not order them to surrender…and surrender to who, exactly – you?'

Salbrinia looked different somehow from the way she did before leaving Hellencia, her skin for one was now a tanned color of opal, while her eyes…her eyes were becoming darker with the faint rising red fire light growing in the back of them.

'***The Sheekan's will surrender to me!*** ' She shouted out with a confident laugh that scared everyone, except for me.

'The Sheekan's must be set free Salbrinia, or Resheen, Spyglass Valley, everywhere will be destroyed!' I yelled in the hope that she would see logic in the peaceful plan.

Behind us Loris was fidgeting in his pocket, while Peron and Ruber started to hide him behind them. This I saw and began to notice that from his pocket he had taken a mirror and placed it on the ground before him. I knew exactly what he was planning.

'By controlling The Sheekan's I stand to win this war, don't you understand Jack? You will finally be able to come home!'

The blinding flash of The Jetstream, the loud virring sound of at least fifty Shadow Runners that were gleaming into The Bad Lands had me distracted from asking her what she meant by her words of home to me.

Jaspro, Norsh, Cadabra, Charadelle, the whole army that made up Spyglass Valley had now in only a few minutes joined us on what looked like the beginnings of a battle, but this was not to be of war or rivalry, it was to be the last stand of peace.

'Salbrinia, I see you have begun the talks without us!' Charadelle said in a calm voice.

'Well of course, as this is my realm you will find that it is my power that rules this plain, Charadelle, not yours. Your powers are useless here…'

Raising a hand and closing my eyes, the air around us began to change ever so slightly, and then, as if by some strange effect The Sheekan that had crashed its way out of the ground now called out to me, as did Salbrinia, who herself tried to use her magic by raising her hands and pointing them at me. It didn't work – nobody else had any use of their powers there except for me. It was at that moment I knew my purpose.

'How are you doing that?' Salbrinia demanded.

'The air is returning to The Bad Lands, Jack Dawson,' The Sheekan spoke in a much softer voice this time.

The drawing of the air had caused The Sheekan's to become more aggressive, but also weaker in their movements toward protecting themselves. As Resheenian's found them docile in many places in Resheen and other places around Chatandra, even, they were recovering from the effects forced onto their lands by something – or someone – very powerful.

I could feel the power in my body lifting the force of the spell, it's pulling of my Elixir being felt in every bone throughout my body. Eventually it began to hurt.

The Sheekan Boneyard

Not everyone was happy that I had some amount of magic, it was true. And though Charadelle and Cadabra seemed pleased that not everyone had their abilities, namely Salbrinia, I had the sneaky suspicion that they, too, were a little green with envy.

'Am I addressing the wisest of The Sheekan Colony?' I called out to the large Creatic that now watched with a cautious eye the many Shadow Runners that stood ready for battle.

'I am Mon'Razi of The Sheekan Hal, you are Jack Dawson, the boy who exists in the middle…you are not Resheenian, you are not Chatandran, either!' It spoke out to the desperate words of Salbrinia demanding that it keep quiet. 'This Witch that you bring here, she has badness in her heart, vengeance in her blood and your death on her mind, Jack Dawson!'

Salbrinia stepped back awkwardly to trip and fall over a large stone that had been moved from its original spot, the tracks of its movement just visible to the naked eye.

'Do not listen to him Jack, he spews lies and spreads the seed of deceit among us all…!'

Silenced by several Shadow Runners who placed a gag over her mouth, I couldn't help but notice that they had all arrived pretty quickly, considering that The Spyglass was still damaged in places where the likes of Charadelle and Cadabra would not be able to travel.

'We will keep her silenced until such a time as she can hold her tongue, until then, maybe we could ask for passage to their Colony. Wouldn't it be more relaxing for Mon'Razi, if he could negotiate from within his own environment?' Charadelle said while having both Cadabra and Jaspro agree with a nod.

'It's your time, Jack, to show that there can be peace among us all here and everywhere else in Chantandra.' Cadabra said with a fonded wide smile that made my cheeks burn red with embarrassment and excitement all at the same time.

Putting this to Mon'Razi, it agreed and asked us to follow down through the darkened plains, while around us there were no more of the large army of Sheekan's that had laid in wait.

William had mentioned a Colony of the Creatic's, though what we saw when reaching Sheelen, the name that Mon'Razi gave for the colossal sized building structures not unlike those of Resheen, was magnificent; darkened walls became seeable by the light tint of The Flares that intermittently cast its sky light across miles and miles of sky, until finally touching the twistles of speckled white dust that was mixed into the walls.

'This is where you all live!' I gasped in wonder of the sight. Mon'Razi stopped and looked around me with a saddened gaze upon its face. I prepared to hear what it was about to tell me.

'This is our Resting Ground, Jack Dawson, not our place of home. Each of these ten thousand structures are for our fallen, our heroes and our families. With so many Sheekan's being killed every day, we are alas running out of land to allow them passage into Sheekpalla, our final resting place before our past kin and those who we will eventually join in death.'

Mon'Razi was quite detailed in his offering of knowledge about his race, even to the point of allowing a select few of us to take a look inside one of the buildings.

The building that we were invited to enter was a little different from all the others there, its structure stretching higher, its walls longer and wider in girth. Upon the doorway which was huge, even for Ruber who had to lower his head, we saw a clawed symbol that was carved into a sign.

'This is the mark of The Razi, my family, my kin…'

'This whole structure is a mausoleum for your entire family!' Cadabra gasped looking up as far as she could to the endless ceiling that showed very little light.

Mon'Razi whispered a quiet "Yes".

Moving on, we were taken past several of the structures to a place where there ran Black Water, which was one of the most precious and rarest waters anywhere; its properties rumored to be from "The First"; descendants of both Resheenian's and those of The Island, a place where nobody here today had ever been, only heard of – or so it was believed.

'May I take some of the Black Water with…!'

Mon'Razi was quick to stop Salbrinia from getting anywhere close to the water that oozed and flowed down from an underground water spring further up on a hill, its eyes showing a look of insistence, while its tone louder than was normal.

'You shall not take The Black Water of Sheekpalla, you are a Witch who will use it against us…!'

Salbrinia objected with a series of tuts, sounds that Mon'Razi was only too familiar with and clearly annoyed at.

'They say that The Black Water runs south of this region, that it travels as far as Fire City, and the lake of Evermore. If this is true, then aren't others, like us entitled to such a gift?' She put to Mon'Razi while walking closer to the isolated water conduit.

'It is our custom here in…'

'***Custom!*** You actually believe you are domesticated, don't you? Even with names you have adopted from false prophets and sublime paradises, it still leaves the question that for many centuries, eons, even. Of how you came to be…here?'

Salbrinia was thorough in her chase for information, though it would appear that she had all but the origins of The Sheekan's in mind. The knowledge was irrelevant to Mon'Razi, but as for the insult, he was already tiring of the woman who was labeled a Witch, by all sides of members.

'The Black Water remains here, if there are any veins that take the water south to any other region, then that is there's to take. Here, we have customs and of those customs, we appreciate our guests to obey them.'

For me, I considered Mon'Razi very wise for the fact that he had actually talked around the circumstances of his reasons for not allowing Salbrinia to take the water. She herself could not believe this Creatic was so intellectually touched, that it knew of reason and accountability; as long as the water was not taken from The Bad Lands, then no tradition or law would be broken as far as The Sheekan Hal Colony were concerned.

'We have an answer to your problem, Mon'Razi, one that you will have to put to your Colony as soon as possible, if that is okay with you?' I spoke up approaching it with a confident look of being accepted.

Mon'Razi thought for a moment, probably of the actual claim that I was offering, one which would certainly beg me for more information about the solution.

'We give you Sanctuary, Mon'Razi, to any place you and your kind want to go!' Charadelle shouted up, her voice alerting all but the people in the next region along. She was loud in her words, dominant and also calid of her presence.

The negotiations, if that is what you wanted to call them were going so well at the beginning, but now, I feared was a time when all the progress we had made so far was going to go to the four winds of Ranoon. If I was wrong, then Charadelle's sudden outburst may have given us the head start on helping The Sheekan's vacate The Bad Lands and begin again as a colony somewhere that they wouldn't be hunted.

Mon'Razi was still thinking, or so we thought, but it was not his mind that was processing the offer, but the entire Sheekan Race; their minds envoped to a maximum tolerance in which to read the others mind. In turn each Sheekan heard exactly what Mon'Razi spoke within his Inner Mind, and in return it transferred the thoughts of the others to him.

'The Sheekan Hal need to know more about your proposal, Jack Dawson. And, if you wouldn't mind not shouting so loud,

Sorceress Charadelle, I think we may have room for one more at the negotiating table in Tanbrix. Come, we have very little time left before the evening stars bring Majuna over our home. We will listen to you – to Jack – and then maybe you, Charadelle, though I believe you know already what is in your heart can never be!'

Charadelle was relieved that Mon'Razi did not take her outburst as an insult, but was very much stunned by its remark on her emotional thoughts that she was at that time thinking.

'***You are reading my mind!***' She cried.

'We read all minds, even Jack's, who is now thinking that The Bad Lands could be a better place, if given enough light. Jaspro is thinking about his friend Jack, how he hopes no harm is going to come to him, and Cadabra…!'

'***DON'T!*** I don't like it!' Cadabra gasped with a flushed face.

Mon'Razi stopped and bowed its head, as if it was feeling shame or some other guilt applied emotion that it now knew it was wrong to repeat others' thoughts aloud.

'Our apologies, Cadabra, we meant no harm. If you would please follow me, over the next hill is Tanbrix.' Mon'Razi was feeling bad about his extraction of all our thoughts that he now knew of us thinking to ourselves.

Reaching Tanbrix we found our mouths dry, our throats thirsty and our bellies hungry from the long exhausting journey. If there was anything, other than The Black Water and Sheekan food around, then it would be some several hundred miles away in any of the chosen direction you cared to point.

'Welcome to our home, Jack Dawson!' Mon'Razi formally announced the sheer spectacle of a vibrant city that had everything and more that The Bad Lands had, except for the dark black scorch that brought the light to an extinguishing cycle of overture. The Bad Lands were dead of everything except for those of The Sheekan's, who could adapt to the many ways in which to survive.

'There is food and water in Tanbrix, Jack, so there is no real need to worry!' Mon'Razi exclaimed suddenly scaring me.

I wasn't worried, not yet, besides, it is said that a fully grown adult the same size as me could last at least two Breakfast's without as much as a Cadbury's Curly Whirly. I don't think it had to be one of those chocolate bars in particular, but I do think that something with yummy chocolate and caramel had to be included for measure. Mon'Razi chuckled to himself as if hearing something funny – was I still allowing my thoughts to parstray the very illustrious memory of chocotoboa's!

'Chocotoboa's, Jack! What is that?' Mon'Razi enquired to a loud rapturous crowd of laughter.

Jaspro and Norsh were the first to cut in and explain in their own words what Chocotoboa was, but of course, it was while they had got past the sweet chocolatey part and onto the caramel, that they each began to feel their stomachs loud and anxious rumblings for the real thing.

Charadelle and Cadabra were quiet this whole time that we became acquainted with the city, some would happen a guess that they were up to something, maybe not up to no good, but certainly up to something that they didn't want the rest of us knowing about.

Finally we had reached Mon'Razi's home, a large pillar of black scorch just like the others, except for the roof that bore the big image of a symbolic attachment to the Colony; Salbrinia had already guessed the height and weight of the insignia as being two-hundred and thirty-six feet in height, one-hundred and ninety-one feet in width, and a staggering weight of ten-thousand five-hundred and twenty-six tons. She was specific.

'The Math is quite easy and straight forward really,' she said blowing her own whistle at her working out the schematics and details of The Sheekan Hal's Prefect of the race.

'Did you know it takes the movement of thirty-two muscles in your face to create a smile?' I asked Salbrinia with a slight arrogant smile beaming across my face.

As if by magic, however, I was toppled to the return reply that had me convulsing with regret at opening my mouth at all.

'Unless you're a Sheekan, which would take seventy-nine facial muscles…or The Baridge Dove, a bird that would require more than ninety-nine of its muscles…'

I couldn't help but switch off the howling voice that she threw out almost speakeristically, rather than from a distance where I wouldn't be needing some form of medical attention.

Entering the house of Mon'Razi, we were very surprised of seeing the plates, the cups and even the cutlery that lay upon a huge table top. It was almost as if the whole structure had been waiting – maybe for this day to come – when Resheenian's and Half Bloods sat down together to speak of peace.

Everyone took a place, which there were not many of, much to the tempered moans of objection by Salbrinia, who came close to being sent away for her behavior. Cadabra had sat down already and found a knife at the side of her plate, one which seemed to be an instrument she knew not how to use. The spoon, too, was of a character she found unfamiliar.

'Food, drinks, delights of sweets and other things that we know you like, Jack, just tuck in and help yourselves.' Our Host encouraged us to begin eating.

A large plate of Majuna Rudikin and Pylosonop Scrim was put onto the table by a Resheekan that was of the Banu'K Clan, it's half developed Sheekanite Mendolos not yet having reached full maturity; as Sheekan was of Resheenian, according to the earlier history books which Cadabra kept locked away safe somewhere in Spyglass City. Legend told of a Resheenian man wandering into a wooded area of Resheen and reappearing in The Bad Lands more than ten eons ago, and what was seen of him was now before us: Resheekan; a mutation of our own design that had been manipulated through many hundred generations of the Creatic Beasts that nearly all of us were afraid of. Which in particular moments of that realization, Loris became a little edgy with fidgeting in his seat.

'The food looks good' I spoke out, addressing nobody in particular, but in a way attempting to put Loris at ease.

Mon'Razi was pleased by my liking of the selection, so much so that he asked the very same Sheekan Banu'K to bring in the Tramsulas Kiake; a delicious build of Ormangino Curep and Achellis Custis, it standing almost as tall as me had our bringer to the lands, Salbrinia moaning under her breath.

'***Tramsulas Kiake, Jack!*** That stuff will make you very sick and do unforetold damage to your teeth…'

'Our delishes are of a very good preparation, I can assure you,' said Mon'Razi, reaching over and taking an ample quarter of the Kiake and stuffing it into his humungous sized mouth.

There was the occasional groan from Salbrinia, her eyes fixed on the Kiake as if she, herself, was actually contemplating on having a portion too.

'The Bad Lands are disappearing, Jack, we are dwindling in our numbers and will not last much longer. The Eastern Fanjin is approaching…we may not survive the fire which it brings.'

The Fanjin was that which The Sheekan's referred to as The Fire, and that which we in Resheen referred to as "***War!***".

I informed Mon'Razi of the plan which was in place, if it was what he wanted to do to save his kind. And, of course, it was this that he had to share with all the other Sheekan's in their telepathic conversation.

'Where will we go?' Mon'Razi asked quite concerned.

I couldn't help but wonder about the question. Salbrinia had mentioned earlier that they could be taken to Hellencia, the one place where they would be safe to wander and be free to do their daily thing. But, even if I was to allow this to happen, there would always be the one thing niggling at my brain: What if Salbrinia made them her slaves?

'Where would you like to go?' I asked quite unprepared for speaking out aloud.

'Home…maybe!' He replied looking up into the air as if he was admiring the darkened sky. 'Home would be a good place to be with our own kind, Jack Dawson.'

I didn't know where The Sheekan's had come from originally, though we all knew someone who did – Cadabra – but she were outside the building. If this location could be found, I thought, then maybe The Sheekan's could travel there and never have to return to the life of being hunted and controlled.

'And where is home, Mon'Razi?' I asked, not really prepared for the answer that was to be returned.

'Our home was once Majesty…'

Mon'Razi spoke of his home, and as he did I began to see what he described as Majestic within my mind. The Winter's cruel, the Summer's soothing. The Sheekan's had been the result of an ancient curse brought upon them by a traveler, Miansun, his journey through light and darkness ascending him to the world where Sheekan Hal and Miansun's kind lived peaceful for so many eons. The soil then was rich with foods, Creatic's such as Ruber's kind, Peron and Salbrinia walked free.

'…Miansun had trodden the ground of a great power, his life taken by a single blow that rested his body by the side of a very young Mudrac, it too killed by the uncontrolled falling of the Resheenian, who for more than one thousand days became as lost as the sound of peace. From the partial elements cast to the lands, he was enriched with the knowledge to teach any Creatic, while his whole self-being was transformed into a half-breed Sheekan. It was the punishment of the powerful ones, not unlike Salbrinia and Charadelle, that he was cursed to stay as hideous and as angry as any other Creatic. Over time he came to accept his punishment and set out to the most northern part of the land, and here he stayed for more than ten millennia…until now.'

My mind was fluxed in a way that everything I had been told was of a dream, the effects of The Black Water and its properties that were so much sought after by Salbrinia, and most probably Charadelle, too. Regardless of this, however, it was the dream that had me suddenly gasp out for air, fresh or old, it didn't matter as long as I could breathe again from the vivid interjection of the story.

'***JACK!***' Mon'Razi shouted out, bringing everyone's eyes toward me now sat gazing into the air with a catatonic look on my face.

'***Resheen…it is…your home!***' I clasped at as much oxygen as I could take in before gasping out my words. 'The Miansun was a Resheenian who brought great shame upon his people, and in turn they banished him to a place where an old woman tricked him into taking shelter from an oncoming storm. He was then drugged by the old woman and handed over to the one person who was betrothed to Vorelee…!'

Everyone sitting, standing, leaning and even lying around listening all gave out a loud gasp at the mention of the name – name that can never be uttered or spoken.

'You should not mention that name here, Jack,' Salbrinia said with a waving finger that reminded me of my Aunt Milly.

'***But yet the story is true!***' I exclaimed, much to that of Charadelle's agreement in the matter of the tales' authenticity and the truth of the facts.

'The Resheenian, Miansun, the one who wandered from the path, he died a very long time ago, Mon'Razi, though there is nothing in the journals that speak of his last resting place.' Cadabra spoke up suddenly, she too, bringing everyone's eyes upon her. 'Or are you saying you do?'

Salbrinia and Charadelle stood whispering together, until the actions of Mon'Razi brought them apart to resume their places.

'Miansun was a name given to him by a Holy Man that lived on The Bow of Celeste near Nasperine, it's translation was…'

'***Brother of the Sun!***' Cadabra interrupted.

Mon'Razi was not angry, not even furious of her rudeness, but he was reactive in a show that saw him walk away for a long moment before returning with a small cover coated sword. It was rested on the ground between both myself and Loris.

'What is it?' Loris asked with a show of rejection to the small metallic object that had rusted over time.

I knew that it was a sword – that much was obvious – but I didn't understand why Mon'Razi had brought it to me. In a moment of sudden awe, Charadelle stepped forward and took up the sword in her hands, she had a strange expression which made Mon'Razi very nervous.

'***This is the sword of The One!***' She whispered softly.

'That it is, Charadelle, the one who was betrayed by the Witch of The Grey Wood, taunted and cursed by the Gods to roam the lands as a Creatic. It's wrought iron steel being of no use to him once his transition had started, the sword was taken to a man in Redstone City, where it was…***blessed!***'

As his final words exited his mouth, Charadelle became scared and nervous all at the same time. She knew that this was no history exhibit, nor was it a short journey down memory lane for Mon'Razi – it was a trap in which she had fallen into. The blade was vibrant with Raven Oil, a deadly substance to many who dabbled in its use, not knowing how much to apply for a maximum effect. For Charadelle, the Raven Oil was deadly, but only in the one true event in which would render its strike.

'*What have you done?*' She cried turning to Salbrinia with a look of sadness, guilt and finally loathing. 'You think that you can kill me? I am Charadelle, and you Mon'Razi, you are weak with the intern of jealousy, regret and guilt. Do not try my patience, for I will…'

Cadabra walked over to her side before giving a short cough.

'You were the Witch that Mon'Razi talks about, aren't you?'

I couldn't believe it. The rest of our group couldn't believe it, either, as they talked amongst themselves in whispers.

Charadelle had been that same "Witch" that Mon'Razi spoke about, but for Charadelle, her story of what was then, was not as is now today. Back when The Miansun was but leaving his thirtieth birthday, she was a much more naïve and monstrous person – The Lady of The Wood.

'I have waited a long time for you, Charadelle, longer than what you would have expected me to wait, and for good reason as to why you are here now,' Mon'Razi revealed, 'take her and put her somewhere that I may look upon her…as for the others, allow them to leave. Jack can stay too!'

Cadabra objected with a stamping fit that brought Mon'Razi to cry out for silence, twirl and twist around in his seat to have rid of the loud screaming voice. Eventually, she stopped.

'Jack comes with us…he is one of us now!' She exclaimed.

Mon'Razi was very surprised that Jack was considered to be one of The Shadow Runners, and even more surprised to know that The Looking Glass was working for me.

'You capture the light of The Jetstream to travel, don't you?'

'The Jetstream helps us move around…'

'I know,' Mon'Razi confirmed with a nodding head. ' The Looking Glass belonged to **THEM!** They were the ones who told us to use it, to understand it and eventually see first-hand what Paradise looked like. History has dealt both Resheenian and Sheekan alike a deep blow, I now know that you're kind have been misguided…'

Salbrinia stepped forward after having opened the black case that contained the Scepter, something that Mon'Razi gave a worried look as its Roarstone suddenly began to glow.

'Hear me, Mon'Razi,' Salbrinia spoke in a strange voice. 'you and The Sheekan Hal will not be lost to the life you have lived within this realm. Take this gift and take it freely as an offer of our friendship. The past cannot be changed…but our fates, entwined and joined together, can change our future.'

Nobody knew what Salbrinia was doing, and I for one didn't understand the reasons behind her offering of the Scepter.

'Isn't that a weapon of sorts?' Loris whispered to me.

Yes, it was a weapon. 'I must admit that this is nothing other than strange, Loris…but we must stand firm and wait.'

Mon'Razi took a hold of The Scepter, its Roarstone becoming brighter and more vibrant than it was when I first saw it back in Hellencia.

Charadelle looked with a face like thunder and an acid tongue temper to boot, she was angry of her sisters gifting, and there was something there that would finally explain everything; The Looking Glass, The Sheekan Hal, Chatandra and the Spyglass Valley world of Lost Boys and Lost Girls who travelled The Jetstream to fight the bad, protect the good and be rewarded with great adventures.

'***You are a fool, dear Sister!*** Ra'Patoose was cast down to Chatandra many eons ago, his Source Light destroyed by The Seekers – The First. You are sealing our fate, Salbrinia to The Sheekan, and with it the power of The Looking Glass.'

In Charadelle's statement she had given both an admission and that of an answer to a questions asked for many of the generations standing around at the time; the scepter was of The Sheekan, not of Charadelle, Salbrinia or Cadabra, but of Miansun, the first to evolve. Acquiring The Scepter of Storms, Miansun was able to defeat the Resheenian-like god and from it he was able to enter The Jetstream.

Giving what sounded like a deep sigh, Mon'Razi settled down in his seat and pointed at Charadelle intensely with a glare.

'You are the one who should be punished, Charadelle...But it would seem that you have someone here who thinks you should be spared an agonizing death. I give you back what has been taken from you, Charadelle, I take back everything that has made all lives here trouble and toil...including you, Jack, if you want everything to be okay?' Mon'Razi bellowed out loudly, turning to face me.

'***Don't do it, Jack, it's a trick!***' Charadelle screamed.

'My Dad...he...!' I couldn't speak clearly for taking big gulps of dread that poised their discomforting weight upon my throat, of which Mon'Razi saw with his own eyes.

'You are saddened because you lost your Father, as a result of this, it was your Mother who felt...Pain!' He spoke up, not the words that I had pinned to my own thoughts while stuttering, but his own words that said almost the same thing.

'My Father died, I was too young to understand...I don't even know what he looked like!' I whispered into a shout that had Mon'Razi lower himself down to face me with a vacant stare that seemed all too odd. Was he going to eat me?

'Charadelle is young in her wiseness to give you the answer that you really seek – You share the same name. You share the same place, too!'

Charadelle looked fluxed, as Salbrinia looked just as bad.

'The Mirror Shard Sphere, Jack, it is your birth rite...'

Charadelle objected with a wave of her hand, a spell casting that did not hit its target, and yet, didn't hit anything at all. It was with a quick turn of Mon'Razi's head that saw the calm and resistant gaze of a Witches attack.

'You drive my patience, Mon'Razi, you should never have called upon The Four Winds in a cry of war!' Charadelle gave a loud cry. 'The Albion Witches were willing to give you Sanctuary, until you betrayed them at Nasperine. Today is the day that you will finally rest.'

The atmosphere was intense. Charadelle stood with both her

hands rising in the air, just as Mon'Razi cried out for her to stop. But Charadelle had mustered up too much power to do anything but unleash a powerful wave of eonic electricity that spewed out of every finger on both her hands.

Mon'Razi cried out, too late to stop the consequences of her actions against him – too late to save her from an unsavory death that happened right before our very eyes.

'***Noooooo!***' He screamed to the reaction of our hands finding the holes of our ears to lower the deafening sound of his voice. The cry was painful, deep and harming.

Charadelle's body, for a moment, looked as if it was floating. In her eyes the blue flame gaze dimmed by a saddened look that finally turned black as sack cloth, before suddenly, her entire body phased into a shimmer which glowed magnificently, as slowly her body dispersed in a show of diamond-like glittering essence. She was gone; nothing remained of the once powerful Albion Witch that had cursed Mon'Razi more than ten eons ago.

My Greatest Adventure

The death of Charadelle was not looked upon as that of murder, though the act which Mon'Razi took against himself being killed, Salbrinia gave a pardon that would make The Shadow Runner's happy, at least. As for Me, the way I saw it all happening, it was no fault of Mon'Razi's, he was only trying to defend himself.

'You did what you had to do, Mon'Razi,' I said quietly.

'Unfortunate are the actions we wield in times of anger and bitterness, Jack, Charadelle's heart was too far past the point of any return to her former self. You, however, I see only good in you, Jack Dawson, and that is why my decision to gift you with one of the most treasured offering's I can give!' He replied with sorrow showing in him as to Charadelle, while raising what looked like a smile.

'***Treasured!***' I gasped out with unintentional excitement that had Cadabra taking a hold of my hand and squeezing it gently.

'Well, yes, of course! I am free of my jailer, and you have brought us all hope…what other treasured gift is there but a young boys only one true wish being granted!' Mon'Razi laughed out with kind intentions. 'There, it is done!'

I looked at Cadabra, and then to Salbrinia, who turned to Mon'Razi with slight confusion.

'What did you just do, exactly?' She asked looking around her. Mon'Razi was amused, and this you could see on his face.

'Jack has travelled far in his quest for The Mirror Shard Sphere, Salbrinia, but he has much further to go…you too!'

Salbrinia, as well as Cadabra were drawn to the statement, but not at the knowledge he had of our quest.

'You know where The Sphere is?' I exclaimed.

Raising himself up to look at the dawning sky through the very center of the building, he gave a slight shudder, before turning back to everyone once more.

'The foothills on the south wall divide of Nasperine's border with the ruins of Caldon, take your bravest of warriors and seek out the Valley of the Dead…!'

Salbrinia cried out a loud gasp of fear.

'Caldon is no more, Mon'Razi, there are no valley's there.'

Her confidence in the confirming of the details showed with a smile that consisted of a half measure of "Truth" and the other half of "Arrogance", but a lot less harsh.

'The Valley of the Dead still remains, though it exists only on The Island, and there you will discover…something amazing!'

With no more talk of Mirror Shards, The Valley of the Dead or The Sheekan Hal Colony, Mon'Razi asked us all to make our way outside into the Rising of the Dawn. It was one of their most honored traditions in which to welcome Sadekta and so welcome in a new day.

After welcoming the sunlight upon our faces, all The Shadow Runners who had entered The Dark Lands with Charadelle and Cadabra, now made their way back to Spyglass Valley, while remaining were just those of my true friends, Jaspro, Norsh, Salbrinia, Peron, Ruber, Loris and of course, Cadabra.

'We is with yous, Jack Dawson, we cans come with yous, can't we?' Loris asked with half glee anticipation.

Looking at Mon'Razi, he gave a low chuckle.

'The Looking Glass is yours, Jack, for you and all of your friends, too. But before you go, there is something that you should know about The Jetstream. Caldon is no place for any mirrors, shards or reflections, it is of no Majuna or Sadekta as it is here in Tanbrix. Travel with caution.'

There were a few questions that I needed to ask, though in my attempt to speak up and ask them, Mon'Razi's voice sounded in my head: Worry not on your journey, for I will be with you.

Leading all of us off back to The Glimf to meet up with William, he and his crew gazed upon us with confusion.

'***Charadelle is not with you!***' He spoke cautiously.

'My Sister is elsewhere, take us to Hellencia and prepare for a journey,' Salbrinia ordered. 'We will not be needing the use of The Glimf once we return to Hellencia, William, we shall be traveling light.'

William smiled. '***The Looking Glass!***'

After arriving back at Salbrinia's Temple, we helped with the packing of food, liquids, equipment and weapons, and then made our way to the Great Hall where both Salbrinia and Cadabra stood waiting in front of a Deity Looking Glass Mirror at least eight feet in height and just as wide.

'Well Jack, you managed to do it. You saved The Sheekan Hal and ridded both evil and war, both, from the dark prospects of destruction. Once again, Chatandra rests with peace, but for us, we are ready to extend that peace...Resheen, The Island and, whether we like it or not, Caldon, too. Are you ready Jack? Are you ready for your greatest adventure yet?' Salbrinia declared lowering a hand for mine.

'My Greatest Adventure?' I gasped.

Taking her hand Salbrinia lifted me up onto the plinth, and then guided me toward The Looking Glass that stood expectant of me entering its Jetstream to our next destination – Valencia on The Isle of Storm...The Island.

The continuing series continues in 2017:

Looking Glass: Lost In Darkness (2017)
Looking Glass: Night Of The Mudrac (2017)
Looking Glass: Chatandra Falls (2017)
Looking Glass: The Majuna & The Sadekta (2017)

Also Coming Soon in 2017

Fairydown
Children Of The Lamplight
Fantastical

Casanova Da Vinci's Big Project:

The Piper's Song (2017)

ABOUT THE AUTHOR

Casanova Da Vinci is a twenty-first-century writer of Literature, some of which reaches into fantastical locations around a single 'Self-Created World'. Having written all his life, bar a decade, he brings together the enriched formula of character and place, as well as introducing his own Tantra-style allure throughout each story and novel.

Previously working on adult oriented books, Casanova Da Vinci has leisurely entered the realms and chasms of younger imaginations to bring a lighter, action packed feel to an exclusive Children's Collection of Adventure and Readership.

Hailing from the UK, Casanova Da Vinci lives in the solitude of his home, while heated by the word processor that never sleeps. Finding inspiration in everyday routines and actions, he is now working on "Resheen", a colossal Epic Story Adventure that encompasses the 1,396 Mini-Novels, Novels and Scripts which makes up "The Lexicon Project".

Be a part of "Resheen", and come visit his Flagship Website at www.gwnonline.com and see what is next in the long 5 year project that is to make History in the Literature World of Writers and Authors worldwide.

Thank You

Casanova Da Vinci

Visit the Author's Official Website @ www.gwnonline.com

2016 © North Gable Productions. All rights reserved.

Made in the USA
Charleston, SC
29 November 2016